PUFFIN BOOKS

THE DRIFTWAY

The Driftway is a strange road, an old road, a road trodden out by feet year after year, winter and summer – a road with tales to tell. Travellers have used the road over thousands of years and every now and then someone does an extra hard bit of living, a powerful experience of sorrow or joy, which leaves a shadow on the road. A message.

On the run from home with his little sister in tow, Paul thumbs a lift on Old Bill's horse-drawn cart, hoping to escape the notice of the police and reach his Gran's house safely. But as they travel slowly down the Driftway, Paul gets to know Old Bill and begins to hear the messages from the past. Some are exciting, some frightening, some sad, but each one contains a special message for Paul.

With its constant and subtle shifts into different times and different moods, this fascinating and strangely haunting novel sets the reader's imagination soaring.

Penelope Lively grew up in Egypt but settled in England after the war. She survived boarding school and had a happier time at Oxford, where she took a degree in History at St Anne's College. She is married to a don, has two children, and lives near Oxford.

PENELOPE LIVELY

The
Driftway

PUFFIN BOOKS

To my grandmother
Beatrice Reckitt
and to Rachel Reckitt

PUFFIN BOOKS

Published by the Penguin Group
27 Wrights Lane, London w8 5TZ, England
Viking Penguin Inc., 40 West 23rd Street, New York, New York 10010, USA
Penguin Books Australia Ltd, Ringwood, Victoria, Australia
Penguin Books Canada Ltd, 2801 John Street, Markham, Ontario, Canada L3R 1B4
Penguin Books (NZ) Ltd, 182–190 Wairau Road, Auckland 10, New Zealand

Penguin Books Ltd, Registered Offices: Harmondsworth, Middlesex, England

First published by William Heinemann Ltd 1972
Published in Puffin Books 1985
3 5 7 9 10 8 6 4

Made and printed in Great Britain by
Richard Clay Ltd, Bungay, Suffolk
Filmset in Monophoto Plantin

I

The shop was bright and hot: it smelt of food, scent and sweat. Big strip lights on the ceiling reached away almost as far as you could see, throwing a hard glare down on to the crowds of people moving between the counters, prowling like hunters among columns of scarlet buckets and tinned dog-food. It was noisy, too, with different layers of sound: the shunt and tinkle of cash-registers lifting above the murmur of voices and the clatter of people's feet. The two children twisted and edged their way among the crowds, knowing where they wanted to go. Paul kept a tight hold on Sandra's wrist: she was small, barely up to his shoulder, and he could easily lose her among all these people. She wanted to buy sweets, but he dragged her past impatiently. They hadn't money to spare for that.

'Not even a sherbet stick?'

He shook his head. 'Not if we're going to get the jug. I told you. If it's less than twenty pence we've got enough. If it's more then we'll have to wait till next week.'

She nodded, docile. She was used to doing what he said.

'When we've got the jug we'll have everything, see. Plates, cups, knives and forks. We can eat up in the room. We won't eat our tea with her any more. We can be on our own.'

He had to shout a bit to make her hear above the noise, so that one or two people glanced at them, but he wasn't bothered about being seen. Their father was at work, and there wouldn't be neighbours here. This shop was right the other side of town: that was why he'd picked it. And

Christine never went there. She said they only sold cheap stuff in those places – stuff that would fall apart as soon as you looked at it. Christine liked good things. She'd bought the skirt Sandra was wearing. Thick, soft cloth. Blue. She'd said it looked nice with Sandra's eyes, and Sandra had been pleased, though she'd tried to hide it from him, and now he hated that skirt. But there wasn't anything he could do about it because she had to wear something, and he couldn't fix that the way he wanted it, the way he'd fixed the room, and the way he was getting all the things they needed gradually, out of his pocket-money, so he could stay upstairs, out of her way, and keep Sandra up there too, and leave her and their father downstairs on their own and maybe in the end not even talk to her any more.

Thinking about her made him go all stiff and clenched, gabbling away to himself inside his head. He always thought about her as 'her'. Never Christine. It was a daft name anyway. Christine. Trust her to have a name like that. She liked people to call her Chris. You wouldn't catch him calling her Chris. Or anything. Just 'you'.

Sandra said plaintively, 'You're squeezing my arm, Paul. You're hurting,' and he unclenched a bit and felt in his pocket to make sure the money was there. Take away the fourpence for the bus fares, and there should be twenty.

They were near the china counter now. The blue and white stuff they'd been getting was piled up in cliffs, framing the face of the bored-looking girl. She wore a green overall like all the assistants in this shop, and she was staring across at him, with glazed eyes that weren't really seeing anything, and her fingers drumming a silent tune on the counter.

Sandra said, 'It's always the same girl. That's the one who sold us the plates last week.'

'I know. Just a minute. I want to look at these.'

If he got a dustpan and brush too, then they could sweep out the room themselves and she wouldn't have to come up there. Maybe he could even lock it – fix on a padlock or something. Then his father would see he really meant it. He'd heard him that time, talking to Christine in the front room, when they thought he wasn't in the house, going on and on about how the boy would settle down in the end and accept the situation, and it would take time and patience, and it was just a shock to him, like, after all this time on their own, and so forth and so on. And Christine saying over and over again something about doing her best, and trying everything she knew. Actually, her voice had sounded very odd, like she might have been crying. Huh ... Anyway, grown-ups don't cry.

He picked up the dustpan. Twenty-six. And the brush another twelve. Well, they couldn't manage that now, but maybe later. There'd be birthday money to come, from Gran, and perhaps Uncle Peter.

He moved over to the china counter, steering Sandra in front of him. They stood looking intently: Paul reading the prices, Sandra picking things up and putting them down again.

'Look, Paul, there's egg-cups too. Couldn't we have some of those?'

'No, we haven't got enough money.' The jug was twenty-five. Too much. They'd have to wait till next week: anger and disappointment gushed inside him.

Sandra was still fiddling with the egg-cups. Suddenly the bored girl stopped looking into the distance and said, 'Leave off, will you, before you break something.'

Paul flared at her. 'She's doing no harm. Anyway s'pose we're buying things?'

She held out a hand, looking six inches above the top of

his head, the other hand fiddling with her hair, chewing something in her mouth. 'Let's see your money, then.'

He scowled back, furious. For two pins he'd get one of the egg-cups, just to show her. But one was no good, and he couldn't manage two. He turned his back, pulling Sandra away.

'Come on. Don't take any notice. She's beastly: foul.' He was in a fury, trembling. 'She looks like her, that girl.'

Sandra turned a surprised face to him. 'Like Christine? But Christine's got fair hair.'

'I said she was like her, didn't I? So she is, see.'

She said quickly, 'Yes, Paul.' They were standing in the middle of the aisle now with people pushing past them. Sandra looked very small and forlorn, just waiting to be told what they were going to do next, and suddenly all his anger went away and he felt horrible, the way he did sometimes. Hating himself. 'Tell you what – let's look at the padlocks. I thought I'd fix a padlock on the door so we can keep all our things safe. Make the room all private, see.'

She brightened. She liked things to do with the room. It was full of her bits and pieces. Beads, and bits of cloth, and pictures from magazines, cards from cigarette packets, old toys: she was like a little bird, nesting.

'Why do we want it private?'

'So she can't come in, of course,' he said impatiently.

She nodded wisely, as though that's what she'd thought all along. She said, 'Who's going to fix the padlock on?'

'I am. We've learned about that sort of thing at school. It's dead easy.'

Well, it probably was. Actually he wouldn't be doing woodwork till next year, or maybe the one after that. But anybody could fix up a padlock.

Sandra said, 'Cor . . .' and put her hand in his. They were at the Do-It-Yourself counter now. Mountains of shiny

8

nails, sleek hammers, screwdrivers, planes, saws, all gleaming in bright colours like sweets. Paul stared, covetous. He reached out and touched the padlocks, picked one up. It closed as soft as butter, with a gentle click, opened again as easy as you like with a tiny silver key. They could have two keys, one each. Sandra could have hers round her neck, on a piece of string, not to lose it. He opened and closed the padlock, lovingly. There'd have to be a chain, of course, and bolts on the door and the door-frame for the chain to go through. The padlock was thirty-seven – far too much to get now, but at least he could work out how much it would all be, and then save up.

He said, 'Here, hold this while I find a chain and the rest of the stuff.' Sandra took the padlock obediently and stood with it clutched in one hand while he moved up and down the counter, searching. He found a chain, but not the right kind of bolt. Pouring the chain from hand to hand, he stared round. They were on the other side of the aisle. He moved over, absorbed, his lips moving as he did sums in his head. Thirty-seven and eight ... Staring at the bolts, he waved at Sandra to come over and join him. Mustn't lose her: the shop was getting more crowded all the time.

He stood, poking a finger through the bolts, still juggling with the chain, Sandra patient by his side. Did screws go straight into wood, or did you have to make a hole first? He fingered the screws, wondering. The chain slipped from his hand and fell to the floor. He picked it up and tucked it into his pocket, his mind on the problem of screws, wood, and whether there were the right tools at home.

Sandra said fretfully, 'Can we go soon?'

'In a minute.' Those screwdrivers were good, with the red plastic handles: he wouldn't mind one of those for his own.

Beyond them, the girl from the china counter stared

across. She stopped smoothing her hair and moved out from behind the counter.

Sandra was fidgeting. 'I'm tired of this shop. Please let's go.'

Eighteen pence. He'd got that much, but it had been for the jug. 'Paul . . .' She was pulling at his hand.

At the end of the aisle, the girl from the china counter was talking to a man in a dark suit. They both looked towards the children.

'All right, then,' said Paul. 'We can't buy this stuff now anyway. I haven't got enough money.' He didn't really *need* a screwdriver, after all. There was one at home, he remembered, in the kitchen drawer.

They began to edge towards the doors. The shop was full now and they had to dodge through the people, knocked by shopping-baskets and push-chairs. At last they came out on to the pavement, and into sunlight. Paul felt irritable and let-down: they had nothing. Waste of time, it had been.

He said, 'Come on. We'd better get the bus.'

The man's hand on his arm made him jump so violently that the voice with it became inaudible, dispersed into the general racket of traffic and people. He pulled back, but the man kept hold, a man in a dark suit, his lips moving soundlessly. Behind him there was the girl from the china counter, still chewing something, but her blank face now weakly illuminated. She stared at the children with as much emotion as she might show watching Indians being massacred on a television screen.

Paul said, 'Here, let go.' The man stooped over him, still holding, and a voice cut through the roar of a passing bus.

'I said, let's see what you've got in your pocket. Come on, now.'

Paul glared, outraged, but his hand went automatically to his pocket. He pulled the chain out and stared at it, stunned. How had it got in there? He began to say things, but the man interrupted.

'All right. You'll have to come along to my office. And the little girl. Thank you, Molly, you can get back to the counter now.'

The girl nodded: a hand crept up to her hair again, patting. 'I seen them last week too. I dunno if they nicked anything, but they was here half the morning, the same two, hanging about.'

The man said again, 'All right, thank you.' He smelled of hair-cream and he'd cut himself shaving: there was blood on his chin, dried black like a tea-leaf.

'The little kid took something, too,' said the girl. She turned and wandered back into the shop, the hand smoothing and twisting a strand of hair at the back of her head.

Paul saw Sandra's fingers uncurl from the padlock, her eyes wide open in astonishment and fright. The man looked down, made an exasperating hissing noise through his teeth. He said to Paul, 'She your sister?'

Paul said nothing, but his eyes agreed.

Sandra whispered, 'You said to hold it, Paul. I didn't put it back, I forgot.'

He wanted to say, 'It's not your fault,' but the man would have heard, and he wasn't going to talk to him. Not if he could help it.

'You should be ashamed of yourself,' said the man, 'leading her on like that. A kid that age. Have you been in trouble before?'

Paul shrugged. People were staring as they passed, turning and looking and then going on. It wasn't their business: they weren't going to get involved in it. A woman with a tartan trolley tutted loudly, and pushed past.

The man said, 'Come on. Back in the shop.' He wheeled Paul ahead of him, a hand tight on his arm: Sandra followed, as though tied to them by a string. They went inside, through the people again, past the counters, tins arranged in bright pyramids, sweets heaped into pinnacles, toothpaste, jewellery, notepads, knives and forks. And padlocks, and chains.

They went through a door at the end of the shop into silence and a corridor with rooms opening off it. The man said, 'In here,' and opened another door, half glass, with black letters on the glass saying 'Manager's Office'. There was a desk, filing cabinets, a couple of chairs. He sat down behind the desk and said, 'What's your name?' looking at Paul.

Paul didn't answer. He could feel Sandra looking at him. She'd be quiet, he knew, unless he talked.

'How old are you?'

Ah, yes, they'd want to know that, wouldn't they. That was the whole point. If you were over a certain age then you were the same as a grown-up and they could slap you straight into a proper prison, just like that. But what was the certain age? Ten? Twelve? More, even? That was what he didn't know. So best just to shut up and say nothing. He ground his teeth together and stared through the dirty glass of the window behind the man's head.

The man said, 'Look, you be sensible, son. You tell me who you are and where you live, and I dare say all we'll do is have a word with your parents and if you've not been in trouble before all you'll get is a telling-off all round and we'll hope it teaches you a lesson.' He pushed the chain and the padlock round the desk with his finger. 'Come on, now.'

And that would be that, of course. That would be just what Christine would like. Just what she'd been waiting for. A thief. Two thieves. Oh no. You won't get me saying who I am. Not even if you torture me. He jutted his chin out and made himself look at the man. Go on, then, hit me, or whatever you're going to do next.

But the man wasn't looking back. He was flicking a lighter at a dead cigarette with one hand, and sorting a pile of papers with the other. He seemed to be losing interest, but of course that would be just a fake. To trap you. Paul stood, waiting.

Sandra said suddenly, 'I want to go home.'

The phone rang. The man picked it up and had a conversation with someone called Ted about a delayed delivery. Then he looked at Sandra and said, 'Sorry about that. What's that you said?' writing something down on a pad at the same time.

But Sandra was silent. She'd seen Paul's face, saying 'Shut up'.

The man was still scribbling. Suddenly he put his pencil down and said, 'Look, I've got all day. You kids ... it's the same every Saturday. Now you know what I'll have to do otherwise?'

They wouldn't put Sandra in prison – she was too young. It would be one of those places they call homes, that aren't. He was beginning to feel a bit sick now, but he could stand there all day, all night too, before he'd say anything.

The man stubbed out his cigarette, picked up the phone again, flipped the dial. He looked over at Paul and shook his head irritably. The phone crackled and he said, 'Hello. Station? Oh, Sergeant Cooper, is it? Selwood's Stores here. Look, I've got a couple of kids here. Yes, that's right. No, I've had a go – you know we don't reckon to bring you out every time – but they won't even give me a name. I s'pose one of your people had better come down and have a word, eh? Yes, I'll be here. Ta, then, cheerio.' He put down the receiver, picked at a tooth with his finger, and pulled the pad and pencil towards him again, frowning. After a moment, he looked up and said, 'You might as well sit down. They'll be a few minutes.'

That was a trick too, of course. Get you all relaxed and off your guard, and then try something nasty. But he was ready for them: they wouldn't get him as easy as that. Paul poked Sandra down into a chair and went on standing himself. The man didn't seem to notice.

They waited. The man scribbled on his pad, read letters, ferreted in a drawer. A wasp crawled up and down the window that needed cleaning. A man in a brown overall came in and said the delivery driver had the invoices ready and the manager said, 'Righto. Tell him I'll be out in half a mo.' Sandra fiddled with her hair-ribbon.

Then there was a knock on the door. The policeman who came in was a woman, which unsettled Paul: he'd not been expecting that, somehow. She had short brown curly hair under her uniform cap, and she looked at him first, and smiled, and then said to the manager, 'All right if I have a word with them here?'

The man got up and said, 'Help yourself, my dear, it's all yours. I'm up to the eyes this morning, anyway.' He came round the desk and they talked for a moment in low voices, the manager picking up the padlock and dropping it on the desk once or twice. He had a different voice for the policewoman, and a way of standing very close to her, but she didn't seem to fancy it because she moved away a bit and just nodded briskly once or twice and then said, 'Thanks. I won't need your office long.'

The manager went away. The policewoman took off her cap and put it on the desk, and then sat down on the corner, pushing a wire tray to one side. She leaned down, rubbed the side of her leg and said, 'You get so you'd like to take your feet off and get yourself a new pair, bashing about on

14

the pavements.' Sandra gave her a look that was almost a smile.

The policewoman said, 'Right, then. What's your name, love?'

Paul stiffened up again. Here we go. He made his mouth into a tight knot and looked over the top of her head.

She said, 'Oh, dear. It's like that, is it?' She took a comb out of her bag and began to tidy her hair. Then she looked at Sandra and said, 'You could do with a wash and a brush up too, couldn't you? And you've lost a hair-ribbon – we'll have to have a look for that.'

Sandra said, 'I want to go home.'

'Right you are. In a minute. I'll take you back in the car. Is your mum at home?'

Sandra said, 'Our mum's dead. There's Christine.' Paul glared, but there wasn't anything he could do.

The policewoman put the comb away and said, 'That's a shame, that is. When did that happen, then?'

'A long time ago,' said Sandra. 'I don't know really. Can we go now?'

The policewoman was looking at Paul. Sandra said in a rush, 'Paul wasn't pinching the chain. He was just looking. And I was only holding the padlock and I forgot to put it back. We were going to get them next week. Anyway, we've got twenty pence.'

The policewoman said, 'Well then, why didn't you say so? You're a daft pair, aren't you? Just standing there saying nothing.' She looked at Paul again. 'Is that it? You put it in your pocket by mistake? You want to be careful about that sort of thing, you know.'

Huh. He knew she didn't really believe that. It was another kind of trick, though he was all muddled now and he couldn't see quite what she was about. But she was about something, that was for sure. Pretending to be all nice and

15

friendly. Like Christine – cooking things she knew he specially liked, and that sort of thing. Trying to get him all mixed up.

The policewoman looked at her watch. 'I don't know about you, but I could do with my tea. Now look, Paul, I want you to be more careful about picking things up in shops, see? People can get the wrong idea. And you've got your sister to look after, too. You don't want to go getting her into trouble, do you. How old is she – six?'

'Seven,' said Sandra indignantly.

'Sorry, love. So be a bit more careful, will you, and we'll forget about it this time. And now it's time you were getting home. This Christine of yours will be wondering where you are. What is she – your auntie?'

Sandra said, 'Our Dad brought her. Easter time.'

The policewoman said, 'Mmn, I see.' She looked at Paul again and said, 'You look a bit flaked out, you do. Peaky. S'pose I give you a ride home in the car?' She got off the desk and smoothed her skirt down. 'Come on, then.'

That was it. That was the trap. Get them into the car, all unsuspecting, and then off to prison. All that stuff about believing him. She probably had half a dozen more police out there waiting. He looked round, wildly. Now what?

The phone rang. The policewoman picked it up and said, 'Selwood's Stores. No, the manager's not in his office just now – could you ring back later, please.' The phone crackled, and she said crossly, 'No, I can't fetch him. Ring back, please. What? Oh, very well, then, I'll leave a message. Hold on a moment, please.' She turned her back on the children and began to grope round the desk for a pencil: her handbag slipped on to the floor and she stooped under the desk to get it.

Paul twitched Sandra out of the chair. He had the door opened and was pulling her through it before the policewoman had time to stand up: as they turned into the passage and began running over slippery linoleum he could hear her saying something.

There was an open door at the end of the passage: beyond, a big concrete yard with lorries and mountains of brown paper boxes, stacked. They went through the door and out into sunlight, past a blue and white police-car parked empty at one side of the yard. Paul looked round desperately: the yard ended at one side in a brick wall, but the other showed an alley leading to a slice of street, with cars going to and fro, and people.

He said, 'Quick! That way.' He had Sandra by the hand.

At the street he looked back over his shoulder: no one was following. Then he looked right and saw a policeman standing farther down the pavement: he was turned sideways to them and talking into the radio hung round his neck.

He'd been right then – she did have more with her. They had the place surrounded: probably that one was talking to her right now. He'd not seen her radio, but she must have had it in her pocket, or her bag. He began to walk away fast in the other direction, wanting to run, but knowing it was better not to.

Sandra said, 'I'm getting a stitch in my side. Why did you run away, Paul?'

'She was going to take us off, wasn't she?'

'Wasn't she a nice lady, then?'

He said shortly, 'No.'

Sandra looked as though she was going to say something, then nodded instead. She said, 'Are they chasing us?'

'Yes.'

'Where'll we go?'

He'd never had any doubt about that. 'We'll go to Gran's.'

2

Gran wouldn't give them away. There was that shed at the end of her garden: she'd let them hide there. Gran would understand: she always did. At least usually. She'd been funny about Christine, mind. The first time she'd come over to see them after the wedding he'd been furious with her. She'd come up the garden path with her face all pleased and smiling. They'd met on the doorstep, and Gran had started on about how she'd always hoped for something like this, and it was just what their Dad needed, and a lot of stuff like that.

It was a slap in the face, just when he'd thought she'd be right on his side. He said, 'What do you mean? Just what he needs? Dad's all right, he doesn't need anything.'

'But he's been lonely, dear. He's needed someone, all these years.'

He stood and stared at her, enraged. Well, when people got old they went a bit funny in the head sometimes, didn't they? P'raps that was happening to Gran. He said, 'How can he be lonely? He's got us, hasn't he?' and Gran had shaken her head to and fro in a sad kind of way, and then she'd gone in and there'd been a lot of talking and laughing and Dad opening a bottle of something and Gran and Christine being all daft and giggly and horrible and in the end he'd gone up to his room and refused to come down for dinner. And Gran hadn't even come up to say good-bye.

They'd made it up later on, just by pretending it hadn't happened. All the same, she'd let him down that time, Gran had.

Sandra said anxiously, 'How'll we get to Gran's? It's such a long way.'

That was true. Gran lived in Cold Higham, and that's miles and miles from Banbury. When they went there with Dad they went in the car, and when Gran came over she came on the bus.

He said, 'We can't go on the bus. They'll be watching the buses. They'll have police all round the bus station.' He glanced back, and there was another of them on the other side of the road, looking straight at him, but he must have been stupid or something because he didn't take any notice of them but just walked away down the road with his hands clasped behind his back. That was a bit of luck: he'd not been concentrating properly, not keeping a proper lookout. You needed eyes in the back of your head. And he had Sandra to think of, too, hanging on to her to make sure she didn't step off the pavement into a car: Dad used to laugh at him, sometimes, and say he fussed over Sandra like an old hen with a chick, but you had to, didn't you, with a little kid?

They'd have to hitch a lift. He wasn't all that keen, really, specially when he'd got Sandra with him, and they'd been told often enough not to take lifts with strangers, but there wasn't anything else he could do. Sandra couldn't walk ten miles. They'd have to walk to the edge of town, so he could pick the right road, the Northampton one, and then just hope someone would stop.

They began walking. Sandra wasn't worried: she pattered along beside him chattering.

'Will we have our tea at Gran's? Are we going to stay at Gran's for always?'

He said, 'Maybe. We'll see.' He wasn't thinking beyond now, beyond getting there. He was frightened, and anxious because here in this part of the town the streets were emptier, and anyone might see them, and he felt all quivery and overcharged inside, like a car engine running too fast. Everything seemed too bright and clear, noises too loud: a car door slamming made him start violently, so that Sandra looked up in surprise. He began to hurry, half-running. There were no policemen in sight now, but he had a growing conviction that other people were watching them. Why did that woman at the bus stop follow them with her eyes? Why did a man in a telephone kiosk stare out at them as he talked?

The shops gave way to houses, the houses became more spaced-out, the town faded into country: a soft, tree-scattered country reaching away into misty distances under a milky autumn sky. It was October, with the air still warm from a sun shining like a copper penny deep in the haze: the trees and hedges flared here and there with orange and russet, dead leaves skirled away under the wheels of passing cars.

Clear of buildings and people, Paul stopped. He said, 'We'll wait here.'

Cars passed. He eyed them nervously: he'd have to be careful which to pick. Best to avoid women – nice motherly-looking women who might ask questions about where they were going, about Sandra, and that kind of thing. A lorry would do, but they roared by so fast, high above him, driven by anonymous, unseen drivers oblivious to his diffident wave.

Minutes passed: no one stopped. Growing impatient, he put his hand out more confidently. And then, suddenly, there was a car pulling up twenty yards ahead. He said to Sandra, 'Come on,' and they were running along the verge towards it.

It was pale blue, newish, with just the driver, a man, leaning over to open the door. He said he was going to

Northampton, asked no questions of them, showed no curiosity, and Paul, relief flooding through him, pulled Sandra into the back beside him.

The radio was playing pop music: the man's fingers on the driving-wheel tapped to the rhythm. There was ginger hair on the backs of his hands, and he had ginger sideboards in front of his ears, and pale hair combed hard back. The skin on the back of his neck was pink below the hair. There was a pile of small cardboard boxes on the seat beside him, an empty cigarette carton on the floor, a stuffed toy tiger nodded on the ledge behind the back seat beside a green tweed hat with a small feather tucked in the headband. Paul, sitting tense on the edge of the seat, observed in silence. Sandra was looking out of the window: she liked car-rides.

The man said, 'Live in Banbury, do you?'

'Yes.'

'D'you know Maple's? The toyshop?'

Paul said, wary, 'Yes. Yes, I think so.'

'I've just come from there. Demonstrating our new range. I'm in toys. Here . . .' He reached out for one of the boxes beside him, flipped open the lid, took something out and passed it back to Paul. 'Have a look – nice little job, isn't it?'

It was a wooden horse on a stand, made of beads threaded on wires. When you pressed a button under the stand the wires collapsed, making the horse buckle at the knees and fall into grotesque attitudes.

'Go on,' said the man. 'Have a go. What d'you think of it? After all, you're the market, aren't you?' He laughed. 'I don't often talk to kiddies, not being a family man.' He whistled softly through his teeth, resting one arm on the window-ledge.

'It's very nice,' said Paul. The horse collapsed and got up, rolling idiot painted eyes.

'It retails at seventeen. No – I tell a lie – twenty.'

Paul put the horse down on the seat surreptitiously. He had to concentrate, keep an eye out of the window: they seemed to be going slowly, stuck in a line of traffic.

'Does your sister like dolls? We're doing a new line this year – the Baby-Smile-and-Cry. Thirty bob. Press it once and it cries: twice and it smiles – just like the real thing. It's got a spring behind the mouth, see – a new gadget. There's one in that box on the floor there – take a dekko at it and give me a professional opinion, what?'

They had come almost to a halt. The man craned out of the window, said, 'They're digging the ruddy road up again, if you'll pardon my French. It's a regular bottleneck, this road. They want to slap a motorway along here, if you ask me.' He lit a cigarette and sat tapping the steering-wheel with brown-stained fingers.

Sandra had taken the doll out of the box and was staring at it without much interest. The man glanced over his shoulder.

'Like the dolly, eh?'

Sandra said nothing and put it back in the box: she'd never cared for dolls. The man looked faintly disappointed. Then he said, 'Oh well, not to worry. It's the mothers buy them, anyway, isn't it?'

They were crawling – five, ten miles an hour. Paul shifted about on the seat, twisted to look out of the back window: the feeling of relief he'd had when they got into the car was beginning to ebb away. Now he felt trapped again, in the glass cage of the car. Anyone could see them: indeed, surely the driver of that car going the other way had looked too hard at the car as he went past? Maybe the police had the number already. Maybe they'd been seen getting in.

He looked out of the window, chewing his lip and scowling. Ahead, the road lifted over a ridge and curled away into the landscape of neat fields, some brown plough, others the pale fawn and cream of stubble, all edged with the ink-green lines of hedges and domed shapes of trees. They were going slowly under a tree now, a huge lime towering above the road: leaves spun from its branches like yellow butter-flies. He made himself follow one with his eyes, spiralling down from the top, because to concentrate on something for a moment eased this drumming feeling of urgency he had inside him, as though an engine throbbed away inside his head. He followed the leaf to the ground, and was sur-prised to see men slumped on the grass verge of the road, at the foot of the tree: tanned, hairy men in tattered clothes, stained leather and rough brown cloth. They must be gypsies or something. There were animals, too, cropping the grass, small bullocks and scraggy sheep. They looked odd, but not just odd in their appearance: their whole presence was strange. It had a distance about it, a remote-ness, and the air around them seemed to shimmer, but then, it was a warm day and there had been mirages in the road, shining like water. And then one of the animals moved suddenly and Paul's attention shifted.

He leaned forward and shouted, 'Mind, mind the cow . . .'

The car swerved. The man said angrily, 'Here, watch it, you nearly had us off the road. What cow, for God's sake?'

It was true. There were no cows, no men. The road stretched away empty between the hedges: empty but for the flash and glitter of passing cars.

Paul said, 'Sorry. I thought . . . I thought there were cows on the road.'

'Not that I can see, sonny Jim. Still, it could happen. Regular neck of the woods, Northants. Myself, I'm for the bright lights. Ah, here we go.'

23

They were past the road-works, out of the traffic jam. The car speeded up, the road sighing under the tyres. Paul relaxed slightly, looked at Sandra, and grinned to reassure her.

She leaned towards him and whispered, 'Are we nearly there?'

'I'm not sure. Yes, nearly.'

He had no idea. The buzzing in his head seemed to have upset his sense of time, and distance.

Suddenly there was noise behind, a banshee wailing that rose above the windy rush of hedges, trees and cars. At the same moment the man said, 'Oy-oy. We've got the law on our tail.'

Paul froze with horror. This was it. This was what he'd been expecting, deep down, all the time. The police car screaming past, forcing them into the verge, the half dozen men closing in on them, the quick, silent ride to wherever the prison was, the door slamming on him, Sandra taken off elsewhere. He made himself look out of the back window: the police car was visible now, a light flashing on the roof. Probably they could read the number by now, knew it was the right car.

The man said, 'Better let them through, I s'pose.' He slowed down, drawing into the side of the road.

Sandra said, 'Is it us they're chasing?'

The man laughed, 'Not unless they've taken to sending patrol cars out after parking tickets – I daresay I've got one or two of those. No – it'll be an accident. Or they're after somebody.'

Paul was thinking wildly. They'd have one more bash at getting away. They put you in prison for that much longer when you'd tried to get away, didn't they? And he'd already done it once, so there was nothing more to lose. Years, it might be. That's just what Christine would like – him in prison for years and years. When the car stopped they'd jump out and make a dash for it over the fields – or roll into the ditch and lie low, like he'd seen someone do once on the telly.

He braced himself to jump, and looked back. The police car was right behind, and then all of a sudden it swung out, overtook them, and was gone down the road. He could hardly believe it. Confidence came rushing back. Whew! That had been a near one. They must be thick, these policemen. Twice now they'd been yards away, and managed not to see them. But it couldn't keep happening. Even now they might realize their mistake, and double back. We're worse off in this car than out of it, he thought.

A sign on the road said Thorpe Mandeville. The man said, 'I need some ciggies. Have to pull in at the shop here.' The car stopped. He got out, saying, 'Shan't be long,' and disappeared into the shop.

Paul said, 'Now. Quick. We're going.' He tugged at the door handle, got it open, and pulled Sandra out after him. She trotted down the road behind him saying, 'I thought we were going all the way in that car, Paul.'

'I changed my mind, didn't I?' He was snapping at her again, worried because the man might come out of the shop, at any moment, before they could get out of sight down the side road. Never mind that, they were leaving the North-ampton road for the time being: he could always find it again later. For the moment all that mattered was to get away from the police car.

He hurried Sandra through the village, glancing over his shoulder every minute, but there was no sign of the blue car, or the traveller, or police. Thorpe Mandeville slept in the afternoon sun, late flowers sparkling against the warm yellow ironstone and red brick of the houses, rooks wheel-ing and plunging overhead, children playing at garden gates. All the same, he was glad to be past the houses and into open country again, following a road that seemed narrower and quieter than the one they had been on before, winding between hedges vibrant with scarlet berries, spread wide from the road along big grass verges. He'd been so anxious and confused in the village that he wasn't certain about the direction any more: the signpost had said Culworth, which seemed vaguely familiar, so presumably this was still the way to Northampton.

They walked on. How far was it now, he wondered? Did he dare thumb another lift? Perhaps it was near enough to walk the rest. At least they could try. He'd had a fright, in that car. Cars were too risky: best to leave them alone if he possibly could.

He glanced at Sandra. She was happy enough, searching the hedges for mouldy blackberries, cramming her pockets with conkers, but she'd flag before long. Sure enough, after another half mile she said, 'Are we nearly there now? My legs ache.'

'Nearly,' he lied. 'Just a bit farther.' He found a tattered paper bag in his pocket, with a couple of toffees, and gave them to her to keep her quiet.

It was peaceful, this road. Hardly a car had passed them in a quarter of an hour. The only noises were the rustle of fallen leaves under their feet and the rumbling of wood pigeons in the trees. Once a flock of lapwings got up from a ploughed field beside the road, filling the sky with sad cries and the tumble of black and white plumage: in a sudden panic he ducked as though under attack before realizing what they were. After, he shook himself angrily: it was like being ill, the way he felt today, everything was twice as loud and twice as bright.

Then suddenly there was another sound: the thud of a horse's hooves on turf. In a moment he saw horse and rider come round a bend in the road, and watched them get nearer and nearer. It was a small, rough horse, more of a pony, and the boy on its back was leaning right over its neck, hands gripping the mane, urging it on. As he came level with them Paul saw his face, and the expression jolted him with a violence that was almost like a physical blow: it was like nothing he had ever seen before. It was the rigid face of fear itself – the white mask, the leaden eyes, the bloodless flesh, and all on the features of a boy about his own age, with straggling matted hair and bare limbs coming from garments that, he later realized, were as incongruous as a picture in some school history book, and he had the same frozen, through-a-glass look that those men by the roadside had had earlier. But as horse and rider careered past him, Paul was aware only of the absorbed, lonely face of the boy who certainly did not see them but swept by and was gone in the direction of Thorpe Mandeville, leaving him startled and stricken at this glimpse of an emotion he had never seen before. What was the matter with the boy? Why was he so desperate? Paul stared down the road, expecting some sign of pursuit, some explanation, but nothing happened. The road lay tranquil in the pearly sunlight, a wood pigeon lumbered overhead among the golden leaves of a chestnut, the hedges fidgeted with the chirp and flutter of small birds. No one came, no one went, except for a tractor crawling in a hidden field, and a woman on a bicycle, carrying apples and cabbages in a pillion-basket.

Sandra had stopped rummaging in the hedges and was beginning to droop, trailing behind him and tripping on the long grass of the verges. She said plaintively, 'I'm not having a fun-time any more. My legs hurt bad now.'

'We'll stop a bit and have a rest.'

They sat down by the hedge, on damp grass beaded with

spiders' webs. The boy, and his startling face, receded from Paul's mind as he was forced to reconsider their own situation. Sandra wasn't going to be able to walk much farther, that was obvious. And that meant hitching a lift again. He scowled, scrubbing the grass with his toe.

There was noise approaching along the road again: a level rumbling this time. A cart appeared, pulled by a brown horse, driven by a man sitting slumped comfortably over the reins, jolting to the rhythm of the wheels: behind, tethered to the cart by lengths of rope, two donkeys plodded. It was a bizarre arrangement, demanding attention. Sandra became alert once more, and sat up, staring.

As the cart drew level with them, they could absorb details. The cart itself was quite individual: it had perhaps been originally an ordinary farm cart, but had now become something more resembling the covered wagon of American pioneers. A crude framework of wood and canvas made it into a home on wheels though far removed from the seaside caravan: pots and pans were slung from hooks on the sides, every space was used for bundles of equipment, strapped, tied, or hung. The donkeys picked their way along the road on delicate feet: in front, the old brown horse plodded with a kind of resignation, ears and tail twitching against the flies, harness shifting and clinking over massive back and flanks. But it was the man himself who caught Paul's attention. He had a long, thin face, with a nose high and delicate as though carved in wood, and a forehead deeply ridged with wrinkles: more wrinkles spread in great fans from the corners of his eyes. He wore an old army greatcoat, hunched around his shoulders, and on his head a battered felt hat was crammed down on hair speckled grey-white like a badger's fur. A thin trail of smoke drifted away behind him from the pipe tucked into one corner of his mouth.

He was strange, unlike anything Paul had seen, and yet not remote in the way that the boy on horseback had been, or, earlier, the men slumped under the tree farther back – the men with sheep and cattle. And as he came close he saw them, turned his head slightly, and raised the whip in his hand in a kind of salutation.

Paul was on his feet almost before he knew what he was going to do. He took a step forward and said, 'I say – could you – could you possibly give us a lift?'

The cart creaked to a halt. The horse shifted from leg to leg, and munched the bit. The man said, 'Travelling, are you?'

'Yes. Yes, we're travelling.'

'Get up then.'

They clambered up beside him, and sat pressed together on a nest of sacks. The man shook the reins and the cart began to move. In front the horse's rump lifted and fell in a comfortable rhythm, the wheels creaked and groaned, the hedges crept by at a walking-pace. There was a feeling of movement in harmony with the landscape, a journeying that followed the natural lifts and twists of the road, gave time to observe a gate, a distant cottage, an unexpected glimpse of a far hill-top, with none of the frenetic rush of a car-drive. Paul felt himself begin to adopt the man's relaxed slump, his legs dangling loose over the edge of the cart.

The man said, 'It won't get you there fast, but it'll get you there so you know you've been travelling, and that's more than most can say nowadays.'

'What's the horse called?' said Sandra.

'Bessie. All brown mares is called Bessie.'

'What are the donkeys for?'

The man hitched the reins over his arm, took the pipe out of his mouth, and began to stuff it with fresh tobacco from a roll in his pocket. 'Donkey-rides for young 'uns. That's how I earns my keep, that, and sharpening knives for the ladies, and the odd bit of scrap now and then.'

Paul said, 'Do you travel about all the time, then?'

'That's right, son, they know Old Bill from Yorkshire to Cornwall, though mostly I stay around the Midlands. Up to Nottingham, maybe, and then down by Worcester and the Severn, and back over to Buckingham. I like to go by the Driftways when I can: there's nothing like a Driftway when you've got animals to graze. A good, wide verge – look at this, now.' He waved his whip at the wide lane stretching ahead.

They jogged on for a few minutes in silence. Then Old Bill said, 'Going far, then?'

Questions . . . Paul drew away so that his arm no longer jolted against the man's side: put up an invisible wall between them: waited for the next one.

But it did not come. Bill was looking straight ahead between the horse's ears, sucking at his pipe with enjoyment.

After a moment Paul said, 'To Cold Higham. To our Gran's.'

'Oh, ay. Well, the road'll take us through Higham right enough.' He gave Paul a quick look from sharp, sunken eyes, as though he were taking stock in some way, and shook the reins on the horse's back. She responded with an irritable twitch of the ears.

Paul said suddenly, 'We're running away.' He spread his fingers out on his knees to stop them clenching and unclenching.

Bill nodded, non-committal, in no way curious.

'We're running away from – from Christine.'

Sandra looked at him in surprise. 'I thought we were running away from the police-lady?' Paul scowled at her.

'Who's Christine, then?' said old Bill.

'She's a person our Dad got married to. At Easter time.'

'Oh, ay. Knock you about, does she?'

'Oh, no,' said Paul, startled. 'No, nothing like that.'

'Got kids of her own?'

'No. No, she hasn't.'

'Can't be doing with them, eh?'

'No, it's not that either, really,' said Paul, lamely. Truth kept creeping in, somehow, like it or not. 'Actually I think she rather likes children.' She gets that daffy look on her face sometimes when she's putting Sandra to bed. I bet she'd try it with me, even, given half a chance. Huh.

Old Bill slanted another look at him, tamped his pipe, and made no comment. Sandra, lulled by the movement of the cart, was leaning against Paul and looked about to fall asleep. They had reached another village – the sign said Culworth – and were passing cottages and shops once more.

Bill said, 'We're not rightly on the Northampton road, here, but old Bessie and the donkeys need water. We'll have to go down to the river.'

'Did you see that boy just now?' said Paul suddenly. 'Just before we met you. The boy on a horse. Running away from something.'

'What sort of a boy?'

Paul described him. Somehow, it was easy to talk to this man: he made no demands, left you to yourself, though the sharpness of his look could be disconcerting.

'It sounds daft,' he finished. 'But he wasn't like anything I've ever seen. It was like looking at someone through a glass window. Like he was kind of locked up in something that was happening to him.'

'Fair enough,' said Old Bill. 'He would be. It sounds to me like the road's been at its tricks again, that's all.'

'The road?'

'This road. The Driftway. This is an old road, son. Older than you or me, or the houses in this village, or the fields round about, or anything we can see now, or even think about.' He took a suck at his pipe, and tapped Bessie's flanks with his whip. 'Get up there, old lady! This is a road that was made when there was first men in these parts, trodden out by feet that had to get from one place to another, and it's been trodden ever since, year by year, winter and summer. Stands to reason it's got a few tales to tell. There's been men passing by here, and women, and children, over thousands of years, travellers. And every now and then there's someone does an extra hard bit of living, as you might call it. That'll leave a shadow on the road, won't it?'

'You mean,' said Paul cautiously, 'that it's haunted.'

'Haunted!' The old man snorted. 'Ghosties and things that go bump in the night! No, son, I'm talking about messages. Look, most living's just jogging along, isn't it? But just sometimes, in everybody's life, there's a time when a whole lot of living gets crammed into a few minutes, or an hour or two, and it may be good or bad, but it's brighter and sharper than all the rest put together. And it may be so sharp it can leave a shadow on a place – if the place is a special place – and at the right time other people can pick up that shadow. Like a message, see? Messages about being happy, or frightened or downright miserable. Messages that cut through time like it wasn't there, because they're about things that are the same for everybody, and always have been, and always will be. That's what the Driftway is: a place where people have left messages for one another.'

Paul sat silent, as they creaked through the village street, and down a sloping hill past the last houses. Sandra was asleep now, a sharp elbow jutting into his side. After a

32

few minutes he said, 'Does everybody get these messages?'

'No. Some never do.'

'Why me, then?'

'Well, look at yourself, son. You're all knotted up, aren't you? In a fair old state. Look at your hands, scrabbling away like a pair of field mice. And the rest of you – all of a twitch. Don't know if you're coming or going. Why don't you take a nap, like the little 'un?'

'I'm not sleepy,' said Paul. 'Actually I'm all right. At least I'm better than I was before – back at the shop.'

They were out of the village now, going under a railway bridge and into open country again. The sun hung lower in the sky now, and the fields were pitted with shadow. As the brilliance of the day began to ebb away the countryside had a tired, worn look, as though the luxuriance of summer had drained it, leaving the gold and copper flaming in the hedges and trees as a last grand gesture: there was already a hint of winter in the bleached grasses that lined the road, and the naked fields, patterned with the swirling curves of the plough. There was a touch of damp in the air, and the faintest wreath of mist curling up the valley.

Old Bill said, 'We'll have a fog tonight.'

'That boy,' said Paul. 'It's funny, but I feel I want to know about him.'

'What's funny about that? So you should. We've all got to listen to other people, haven't we? Find out what it's like for them.'

Paul said nothing. He looked at the old man for a moment, and then away, out into the spread of fields and sky.

'Or what it's been like,' Bill went on. 'To my way of thinking other people's not just the few blokes you happen to come across. It's them you never knew as well, because they're in other times, or other places. Because they're the

33

same as you and me, aren't they, in the end? You've got to want to know about them, unless you're going to spend your time shut up inside your own head, and there's quite a few like that, more's the pity. But this road'll talk to you if you're the kind of person wants to be told things. There's some don't care one way or the other: they're not bothered. They'll live out their lives shut up inside themselves, just looking straight in front of them like old Bessie here, between two blinkers. All right, if that's how they want it. But it don't suit me. Or you, I'd hope.'

They trundled on another mile or so, and began to climb a ridge. As they reached the top Old Bill said, 'Over the other side they call the valley Danesmoor. On account of there being a battle fought there between the Saxons and the Danes. And then later there was another on the same place. In medieval times. The Wars of the Roses.'

'How do you know all that?' said Paul.

'Ah. I've read books in my time. I told you it don't suit me not knowing about things. Know nothing, and you are nothing. Though it's not all in books, mind. Now that's history, what I've just been saying. But to my way of thinking history's just another word for messages. You can dress it up in fancy language, but in the end it's people sending each other messages, isn't it? Trying to find out about each other: tell each other how it is. Eh?'

'I s'pose so,' said Paul. They had reached the top of the hill now. Through a gateway the valley beyond was spread wide to the sky, fawn-coloured fields reaching up the slope to meet a blue-green drift of woodland, a stream along the bottom edged with brilliant trees, rowan, beech, and crab-apple, cows moving peaceably on a stretch of grass spattered with the deep green of rushes and marshland. A flock of rooks swung across the golden sky.

'There,' said Old Bill. 'Men have died there. There's a

thought for you, son. You just think about that.' They stood for a moment, staring. There were scarlet berries on the trees by the stream: they glowed, caught by the dying sun. 'We'll get down to the water. Let old Bessie rest herself a bit, and maybe have us a brew-up ourselves, eh?'

3

There was a bridge over the Cherwell, at the point where another road joined their own at right-angles: an old, stone bridge taking the road across the stream, with the water lapping softly at worn piers. There were knobbed teazles on the banks, and faded pads of water lilies shifting with the current. Old Bill unhitched Bessie and the donkeys and turned them loose to drink and graze. Then he set to and built a small fire, conjuring it as though by magic from leaves and brushwood: a kettle was put on a trivet to boil, and they sat down on the grass. Sandra, swathed in sacks and an ancient coat, was curled up asleep at the front of the cart.

The rising mist lay along the river like a scarf, tracing its course from west to east, and marking the tributary stream that wound away along the valley to the south, hidden among the rowan and crabapples. It was as though the air gathered and intensified over the water: elsewhere, on the higher ground along the ridges, the sunlight still poured down on shining stubble and bright brown earth. The damp felt like a cold hand gripping the skin: Paul shrugged down into his windcheater, staring at the red glow of the fire and the flames that curled and spread around the blackened base of the kettle. He felt a little tired now, but calmer: he no longer listened for the following wail of the police car. In the peace of this place it would have seemed like an intruder from another world.

Old Bill stirred the fire: sparks arched up and fell back into the ashes. 'It wasn't always as quiet as this here,' he said, 'it's seen a lot of coming and going, this place. See that road, going back from the bridge up the hill?'

Paul looked up. It was a quiet, empty road, more of a lane but set again between wide grass verges, reaching straight up the hill and vanishing into the skyline. 'Yes.'

'That's called the Welsh Road, that is. On account of it was used in the old days to bring cattle from Wales to sell at the markets in these parts, at Northampton and at Banbury, and farther, too, in London and the south. It's another Driftway, like the one we just come along. They meet up together here, at the bridge. There'd have been a lot of traffic here, in old times.'

Men, and sheep, and cows . . . Paul said, 'Oh. Oh, I see now. A driftway means a road for driving animals along. Now I get it.'

The kettle had begun to sing: steam belched from the lid, and mixed with blue smoke and heat shimmer above the fire. Old Bill was setting mugs on the grass, and twists of paper with tea and sugar.

'Farther back – on the other road – before we met you, I saw some of them, I think. I thought the car was going to hit a cow, and then there wasn't one.'

'Very like,' said Bill, 'very like. We'll let the little 'un sleep. She can have her tea later.'

They sat, nursing the hot mugs in their hands. The tea was black, sweet, and strong so that it caught the back of the throat and dried up the mouth. But it was good. Old Bill seemed to doze, slumped against a tree-stump, his chin tucked down into a scarf, the pipe in his mouth. It was very still, as though any breath of wind had been quenched by the thickening mist: there was no sound except the soft tearing noises made by the grazing animals, and no movement, even the drifting leaves lying in frozen, stiff-looking piles on grass and road. The world seemed suspended, timeless.

Something, half-seen in green shadow under a thorn bush, made Paul turn his head. A shape, an outline, an old sack flung down, perhaps, a pile of brushwood, a dog, even, huddled into the grass . . . He peered, uncertain, wary, and then the thing moved, made no sound, and it was a boy.

It was the boy who had ridden past them earlier. He crouched now under the hedge like a beaten animal. He was there, the shape of him, and the grass crushed under his weight, and the trail even of his breath in the cold air, and yet he was immeasurably far away, as though seen through a telescope. Paul, staring across the yards between them, knew that if he moved towards the boy he would never reach him: the distance between them was of a different order, awesome and mysterious. He was here, and yet so far away that to hold him was an effort of concentration, an effort to focus on that one spot of grass and shadow. And as Paul watched, motionless because somehow he could not move – it was as though he were held where he was, with the mug of tea in his hand, halfway to his lips – between him and this other boy there was speech, though Paul never once opened his mouth, and afterwards, later, he had no memory of a voice, whether it was loud or soft, or how it sounded, but only of the telling. And all through the telling, however long it took, minutes, or hours, or no time at all, it was as though he saw nothing, not the road, or the bridge, or the cart with Sandra asleep, or Old Bill, but was just an ear listening, absorbing the tale that came to him through the mist from that outline of a human form there just over the grass. This, then, was a message: a message that could beam like a light through time itself.

I dreamed last night of bloody suns, not one, but many,

38

spinning through darkness like balls of fire. And when I woke, and stepped from the hut to go about my business in the fields, the clouds to the east above the trees were rimmed with red, and the sky blazed as with fire, and I was afraid. For of all things we fear most that which we do not understand, the dark creatures of the night, and the foul fiends of moor and lake, dragons, monsters, and spirits, and the signs in the heavens which are a warning of what must come, if we knew only how to read them. And so, in all this day of terror and of weeping, I was most afraid at that moment, when the sun was barely risen, and the world silent, and the people yet asleep, and the oxen tethered, because the fear was in my mind, and not yet in my body, and I had no arms against it. Later, with my spear in my hand and death on every side, my fear was turned to rage, and rage to strength, for all men know the fury of battle, and death is with us always, and these things we understand. But now, when the slaughter is done, and the fires burned out, and the Norsemen are gone, now I am most afraid, for my people are dead, and I am alone, and I have no hearth, nor kin, and without those things I am nothing, so that it were better if I, too, lay cold by the stream there like my father and my brothers.

I am Cynric, son of Cynwulf. My father is a free man, a ceorl of Aelward's people. Our homestead and our plough-lands lie in the clearing there, above the moor and the stream: the land is good and does not flood. When things go well for us there is enough here for man and beast: barley springs from the black earth, the grass swells the cattle and turns to milk and meat, and the forest gives us fuel and timber and mast for the swine. Our people have been long here: they cleared the forest in olden times and divided up the holdings, and worked the land and made it good. Always we have had the fear of troubles: pestilence, and famine, fire, the wild beasts of the forest. But in the time of my father's father there began a greater trouble, for the Norsemen came from the sea in their long ships, and ravaged our country with fire and sword, and now they are settled in that part of our country which lies beyond Watling Street, around Northampton and beyond there, and they hold that land and take taxes from the people, and they live there according to their custom and worshipping their own gods. But in these times there is not always strife between Saxon and Dane, for the Norsemen have learned that we are grown strong in Wessex, and our burhs are many and can withstand the fury of the attacking horde, and so of late there has been peace between us, and traffic in goods and cattle, and men say even that some of the Norsemen turn to Christian worship, thinking that our God must be stronger.

But today are we forsaken, for the church lies in ashes beyond the hill, with all the huts and bothies, and the ploughs, and the women's looms, and all that we had, our fields destroyed and our cattle gone, driven off by the Norsemen.

We called upon God to help us, before the battle, but he heard us not. And there were those too who made sacrifices to the old gods, to Woden and to Thunor at the shrine in the clearing, but they too have forsaken us.

I will tell you how all this came about – this day of bloodshed and of weeping. When the sun was up my father, Cynwulf, told me that I must go to Culworth, where my father's brother has his holding, and fetch back from him the oxen that he borrowed from us when his plough team fell sick. For this is the springtime, when the green mist comes upon the fields and forest, and we must turn the black earth, and plant the seed, and charm the plough and light the need-fires so that our crops will be good and there will be bread enough for all. The road to Culworth goes over the ridge and through the forest, where the grey wolf slinks, and the dark spirits of the wood, but I am a man now and cannot show fear of these things, so I prepared to go on my way, but I asked that I might take the horse, that the journey should be quicker. I rode forth from the tun, leaving my mother and the other women busy at hearth and loom, and the men already gone to fields and pasture, and I rode towards the sun, through the ploughlands and over the moor and into the forest. The distance is not great, but the road is heavy from the winter rains in many places, and the forest is thick, so that from time to time the horse could move no faster than a walk, and then I watched the trees for what might come forth, but the wild beasts kept away and I saw nothing but young deer. Presently the land began to fall away and I knew that I had crossed the ridge and would soon reach the clearing and the settlement of my uncle's people, and I was glad. And then, through the thickness of the trees, I heard sounds, shouting and cries, and there came too the smell of burning, and I was afraid for I knew all was not well at the settlement, but I did not know what to expect. So I rode on the faster until I came to the edge of the clearing, and then I saw a sight that struck terror to my heart, so that I clung to the horse and shook like a woman, and wept.

There was red fire like flowers where the huts had been, and the grey sky swallowed up the smoke, and the women were running and wailing, far away on the hillside, and there were men lying on the brown earth and everywhere the Norsemen in their war dress, with their great horned helmets, and the round shields, and the shining axes flashing in the sunlight. And then I knew that they must have come like thieves in the night, silently and without warning along the road that goes to Northampton, and our people had no chance against them for they are few and weak, and I knew I must turn and go quickly back to warn my kin, and the people beyond at Wardington and at the other places, to take up their spears and prepare to defend themselves and their homes against the murdering Danes.

I rode through the forest like one possessed by a demon, with a great fear in my soul, for I had seen that the enemy were many, well-armed and horsed, and I knew they would not stay long once their evil work was done, but would ride on in search of more plunder. I rode by the outlying places crying out the fearful news to the people there, so that the men came running from the fields to drive the cattle within the tun, and to get ready their weapons and prepare to fight, and they sent a man to ride to Wardington, for there are many ceorls there, and Beornoth the thegn, who is a warrior and fought with the King against the Danes five winters ago, and was one of the King's companions.

And then I turned and rode back over the moor once again towards the homestead, with many glances backwards to see if the Norsemen were come through the forest yet, but there was silence and stillness, with only the trees spreading like a mantle over the earth as far as a man could see. And the great eye of the sun shone red above me, and I remembered my dream, and knew it had been a sign.

We lost no time in getting ready our weapons, my father and my brothers and the other men of the village, for every Saxon ceorl is used to serving with the fyrd when needs must, and keeps ready sword and spear. The cattle were driven within the enclosure, the women and children brought to the huts, and all the while the thought was in every man's mind that we were few, too few, and the Norsemen were many. And then, as the sun climbed in the sky, we heard a noise of men and horses from the west and we saw that Beornoth, and the men from Wardington, and men from the thorp too, were coming over the hill, and we understood that they meant to join with us and fight the Danes on the moor, which they must cross before they could reach the settlements, and in this way we would be stronger, and our spirits rose and for the first time we felt hope.

But when the Danes rode out of the forest we saw that their numbers were even greater than we thought. Like a river they were, a river of men flowing from the trees and along the track, and above them and beyond we could see the smoke rising where the huts still burned at Culworth, and we were seized with a great anger, and the anger gave us courage, so that our hands gripped our weapons as we waited for them, and all was silent on the moor save for the cries of the marsh birds, redshanks and plover.

We chose for our stand the piece of rising ground to the west of the stream, for you can see from there the track from the woods, and the road to the north, and the hills all around, and we waited for them to come up the slope towards us and then we fell on them with a great cry, and I saw only the bright suns of their shields as they came upon us, and heard nothing but the crash of axe and sword. The whole moor was filled with the shouting of men, and I fought among them, beside my father Cynwulf, and my brothers. I saw my brother Edric fall to the axe of a Norseman, a man so huge he seemed a giant, howling like a wolf in the rage of battle, and all around I saw my kinsmen fall, for the Vikings were many, and skilled in battle, so that as the leaders grew weary they fell back and more came up to take their places. And all the while those of us who yet escaped death were driven back and back across the moor towards the village, so that the attack we had sought to make upon them was become a retreat before their greater numbers, and while we fought on we knew in our hearts that it was useless, and the end was near.

Many times in that hour I thought I should die: many times I turned to see a Viking axe raised to cut me down, and stepped back so that the steel whistled through empty air: once I stumbled and fell so that I lay helpless on the ground, with nothing but my shield between my body and a murderous sword, but the blow fell crooked so that I rolled aside with my body bruised and shield half-crushed, but still alive. Once an axe-blow gashed my arm, so that the blood flowed, but I felt nothing, though the arm grew numb, and I could use it no more. I saw Beornoth fall, and many with him, and many Norsemen among them, till the moor, the place of silence, the place of reed and stream and wild creature, was become a field of slaughter, with men lying still under the wide sky. And at last we few who were left behind turned and fled into the forest, for we could fight no more, and the end was come, and the sky grew dark again with smoke as they burned our homes, and drove forth our cattle, and took what they wanted from us, and left the rest in ruins.

The women and children ran off into the forest, as they saw their men fall before the Danes, for it is known that in their fury they spare no living thing. They wait in grief among the trees: they, and we few who are left, old men and boys, for it was the strength of our people that fell before the Danes, the men of Edgcote, and of Wardington. Night is not far off: we must bury our dead before darkness comes, and the beasts of the forests. They are with the gods now, my father and my brothers, and I am alone in a cold world and I would that I lay with them there on the moor, with my face turned to the sky where the bright sun falls below the hill.

*

44

There was something hot on his knee: the tea had slopped and was trickling down his leg. Paul took a sip and put the mug down on the grass. The voice which was not a voice had stopped, and the boy was gone with it: the density which had been the shape of him against the hedge and seemed to shake or quiver, and then to recede and recede as though it travelled unimaginable distances, and then it was no longer there. And all the time of the telling had been nothing, for the tea was still scalding hot, and old Bill in the same position, and the horse in the same place, chumping grass.

The old man stretched, sucked his pipe and took a gulp of tea. 'Time we were moving on, son.'

Paul said, 'What you said just now – about those messages, from other times – well, I think it happened just then. There was a boy, and he told me all about a battle, and all the people in the villages being killed. I mean, he told me somehow, but I didn't exactly hear him, more just knew about it. I felt it. Felt it all going on – the people so scared, and the fighting, and the emptiness when it was all finished.'

Old Bill said nothing, but his sharp eyes glinted, deep in the wrinkles of his face. He began to spread the ashes of the fire with a stick.

'He was so lonely. His father was killed, you see, and his brothers, and he felt he should have been too. And he hadn't got a home any more. He felt everything had ended.'

'Oh, ay.'

'But he was talking about the places that are here now. Culworth, and the others.'

'Places go on. They last a sight longer than people do. And the names of places. They're old, always. From old times. From the people that made them first, cleared the land and that.'

45

'He talked about that,' said Paul. 'About his people clearing the forest, but long before.'

'He'd know about it. Not from books, like us, but by people telling each other. Knowing it matters to know what went before. The names of people, and what they did.'

The mist was moving now: skeins of it rolled across the road and swept in a white tide over the fields. It seemed to breathe up from the water, the stream running below the bridge.

It's the same stream, Paul thought, the same stream the boy talked about. He heard it like I can hear it now, and saw that long flat hill just the same as I see it. Aloud, he said, 'It all happened out there, beside the stream. It really did happen, I know that. It was all true.'

'And you hadn't ever thought about old things being true before. Thought they were done with, and that's all. It's a bit of a jolt, eh?'

Paul nodded.

'I'll tell you something else, son. I bet it's a while since you forgot yourself like that. Thought about something else.'

Paul stiffened, scowled. What did the old man mean? Was he getting at him?

'Don't take on. It's true enough. You think the whole world's looking at you, but they're not, you know. Mostly they don't even know you're there. Come on, we've got to get moving. You get those donkeys hitched up while I see to old Bessie.'

The donkeys' coats were all beaded with the mist, the ropes wet and clammy. Paul tugged at their halters and they followed him, docile, while he knotted them to rings at the back of the cart. Sandra woke up and said she was hungry. The old man gave her biscuits and an apple, which she inspected critically and then ate as though she had never eaten before.

'She's got an appetite all right, your little 'un,' said Old Bill. 'You know something else, son? The first time you get yourself worked up about other people – strangers, people you've never known, never will know – that's when you're beginning to grow up. You're learning. Mind, some people never do, and they're the ones you want to look out for. There's a lot of harm can come from them.'

Paul shook his head irritably: it was all very well, going on like that. It sounded all very clever – no, not clever, because the old man wasn't a clever kind of person – more *right*. Wise, or something. But it was a bit annoying. What was all this about thinking of yourself? Did the old man mean he was selfish or something? Well, that was cheek, that was. He didn't have a clue really what it was like to be Paul, for instance, did he? What it was like to be all settled, with things going along quite nicely, and then suddenly everything being turned upside down and *her* being there. They'd been all right, hadn't they? Dad could cook fine – lovely stuff like bangers and chips, and kippers, and porridge for breakfast. And Gran came in to do the washing and that, and he cleaned his shoes and Sandra's and saw Sandra to school and fixed her hair in the morning. They didn't need Christine, did they? Gran was quite wrong about Dad: he wasn't lonely. How could he be?

The gabbling was beginning again inside his head: going on and on, saying all the things he never said out loud. Old Bill's voice cut through it sharply.

'Come on, son, up you get. We're off.'

The cart lumbered up the hills again, Bessie blowing and flattening her ears, regretting the lush grass by the stream. The air was clammy with mist, and there were no longer any edges to the world, only a gradual disappearing of trees and fields into whiteness: Paul drew the old coat and the sacks round Sandra. She caught colds easily: you had to watch out for that.

She said, 'Are we nearly at Gran's?'

'Nearly.' Anyway, this fog would make it more difficult for the police to find them. Or would it? He stared ahead uneasily: a police car could come popping out of that whiteness and be on top of you before you knew what was happening. And then that would be that. But if they could get to Gran's then they were all right, because, and he'd worked this out carefully, the police still didn't know who they were, and there wasn't any way they could find out. And once they were at Gran's there they'd stay. Sandra too, and if Dad wanted them back he'd have to come asking on his bended knees, wouldn't he?

Old Bill said, 'Staying permanent with your Gran, are you?'

'Yes.'

'Getting on, is she?'

'Getting on? Oh, yes. Well, she's pretty old, I s'pose.'

'But she won't mind doing for a couple of kids. Cooking and washing and that.'

'Of course not,' said Paul angrily, 'why should she?'

Bill said nothing. They creaked on in silence, along an empty road. Although the time must now be early evening, it was very light: the mist had its own brightness, shining white, rolling back before them all the time to reveal the smoky shapes of trees tipped with bronze, the colour flaring in wild contrast to the white background. The hedges, too, smouldered with colour – orange and yellow and a sharp brown. They seemed to move in a globe of colour through a blank world, a globe that contained only the cart, and portions of road, grass and hedge in front, behind and on either side. All beyond was hidden, and sound, too, was

48

masked so that they heard nothing but the noises they carried with them, the rumble of the cart, the clop of Bessie's hooves and the lighter titupping of the donkeys behind.

Paul said, 'She won't mind. I'm sure she won't.' It must get lonely, being on your own like that, when you're old. Funny, he'd never really thought about that before. About Gran as Gran: only about Gran in connection with him. Gran coming over on Sundays and doing things Dad hadn't got around to doing in the house: Gran in her cottage making a special tea for them when they went to see her: not Gran by herself. She wouldn't mind them coming – of course she wouldn't. He'd always got on with Gran: that was why it had been specially horrible seeing Gran laughing and chatting and getting on with Christine. She shouldn't have done that. Nobody'd understood, nobody at all. There'd been Mrs Jackson next door, who he'd always liked, trying to say things to him. 'Can't you give her a chance, dear?' Huh. Nobody'd asked him if it was all right for her to move in, had they? 'It's not as though she's some silly young girl, dear. She's a real homely person.' Well, if homely meant making good meals and keeping things clean and that, maybe she was. 'And warm. You can see she needs to make a home. It's wonderful to see your Dad like he is these days.' Well, Dad was just the same as he'd always been, wasn't he? Or was he? Was he maybe a bit different? More talkative – he'd always been a quiet kind of person – less worried-looking?

Matter of fact, I'm not sure, Paul thought. I kind of don't notice other people when I start talking to myself in my head about Christine, getting all fed up . . . What does Dad look like these days?

'Won't your Dad have something to say about you clearing out like this?' said Bill, making him jump. 'I'd have got a tanning from my old man.'

'It'll be all right,' said Paul, flushing, disliking himself. 'We often go to Gran's.' Well, that was true, wasn't it? Not by themselves, though. Not without telling anyone.

'Ah, you've put me in mind of a time when I was a lad around your age,' the old man chuckled. 'I'd got myself in trouble – I forget what it were all about now, but I'd had a right old barney with my mum, and my dad took the strap to me, and I was that sour about it I thought I'd clear out once and for all. Teach them a lesson, like. Go to London and make my fortune, that kind of thing. Come back in ten years' time and see the tears in their eyes. So off I went, and I walked about twenty miles by my reckoning – about two in fact, I daresay – and by then I was that hungry I thought I'd go back and see how sorry they were. And in I marched, thinking I'd get such a welcome, and they hadn't even noticed I'd been gone. "Now then," my mum said, "don't you go coming in here and getting under my feet."'

'Did she?' said Paul stiffly, and looked away.

A density behind the rolling fog assumed shape and became a cottage, and then another one, and finally a row, with windows glowing orange. A soft outline at the edge of the road hardened into a parked car: a black shadow became a cat, sitting humped-backed on a garden wall.

'Where are we?' he said.

Bill shot him one of those sharp looks from the corner of one eye.

'Culworth. You'll not mind if we stop a few minutes? I'd like a pint. We'll pull up at the Red Lion.'

4

Bessie turned into the yard of the Red Lion without so much as a twitch on the reins from Old Bill: this was a regular port of call. The pub was an old building, its face turned to the village street, its rear opening on to a cluttered yard, half car park, full of crates and barrels. Bessie was hitched to an iron ring in the wall and provided with a nosebag: the donkeys went to sleep on their feet, eyes half-closed, twitching their thick felt ears from time to time. Bill vanished into the pub, saying he'd not be long.

The children sat on the cart. It was quiet in the yard, except for a dog eating a bone beside a dustbin, and gusts of sound when the pub door opened: men's voices, and the chink of glasses. Sandra grumbled once or twice that she was cold until Paul found more sacks, and a motheaten blanket, and then she buried herself in them, with only a bony knee sticking out, and dozed off, murmuring from time to time.

Paul sat still, watching the light fade over the roof and the corners of the yard grow shadowy. Car headlights flickered past at the end of the alley leading to the street, and a television set quacked from an open window in a cottage behind. His mind was empty: scoured for the moment by exhaustion. He did not want to sleep, but simply to sit for a while and forget everything: the police, Gran, his father, Christine, himself.

And then someone began to laugh, quite near, just by his shoulder, it seemed. He turned his head, but could see nothing. It was a chuckling, mocking laugh: the yard seemed full of it, bouncing off the dark walls and running up the drainpipes. He said cautiously, 'Is anyone there?' and the laugh turned to a snort, and a snigger, and then a voice began to speak, a nudging, confiding voice, a voice that was like a tap on the shoulder from a stranger, a voice so compelling and with such substance that Paul ceased to search for its owner in the twilight places beyond the cart, but knew that once again something came to him from distances he must not, could not, investigate, and sat hunched there in the gathering dark, alert, intent, and glad.

Oh, but I'm a sorry fellow tonight (said the voice): a sorry fellow indeed, for there's none so sore as he who has a fortune in his grasp, only to see it snatched from him, and that as the just reward for his own damned knavery. For it's a rascally tale I have to tell, traveller, and I trust you've a strong stomach, for it's a tale of trickery, and duplicity, and craft and guile such as puts the human race to shame, and I most of all, and the more still when I tell you that I care not a jot, except that I'm tricked with the rest of them, and stuck here to sweat out my time as stable-lad and coachman's boy, when I thought to be halfway to the taverns of London, with gold in my pocket and a gentleman's finery on my back. For I am hoist with my own petard, but I'm not such a numskull as I can't see the joke of it, and there's nothing else I'll get out of today's work now but a good belly-laugh, so I might as well have that and be done with it. But hear my story, and judge for yourself who's the loser, for it's a pretty fable of do-as-you-would-be-done-by, and I'll be damned if there's not a moral about it somewhere.

My name's Jack Trip, and I've worked in the stables here these ten years, since the day the innkeeper took pity on a poor consumptive creature in the village, dying, and without a husband to her name (or never had one, to be sure), and said he'd give bed and work to her orphan son, and so he did, and so he does to this day, for he's a Christian fellow, though I daresay you're thinking him an uncommonly bad judge of character. For I'm indeed that orphan wretch, and a poor thing I turned out to be, to confound all the stories of orphans and foundlings come to fame and fortune through excellence of character or refinement of spirit. The only distinction I ever showed was an excellent talent for avoiding work, whether it were by hiding from the ostler till he bawled for me in vain, or snivelling to mine host's good lady, who's a soft-hearted soul, of cramps in my stomach or pains in my head. Thus, and by putting up a fine show of employment while at the same time achieving as little as I could, I've managed to spend my time tolerably well, and fill my belly to boot, for there's no place like an inn to provide for your bodily needs. I reckon that with a trifling rearrangement of my lady's larder I can eat as well as any gentleman travelling to London from his country place, and I've grown a nose for a ripe cheese or a nice-cooked leg of mutton as refined as any Bishop, not to mention a palate for wine that wouldn't shame a Lord.

So, all in all, I began to feel myself cut out for finer things and the more so, since as you'll perceive, the constant rubbing up against a better class of person than your Northamptonshire bumpkin has given me the chance to filch some of their manners as well. Indeed, I can speak very gentlemanly when I wish, and turn a pretty phrase, with none of your yawning country vowels. But the taste for a better station in life never did anyone any good unless he had the fortune to provide it, and a fortune I had to have, by hook or by crook, by fair means or foul, for I was grown impatient. True, I'd never lacked for ready cash: an inn can be made to leak coins as readily as it leaks mutton chops and pork pies for one who knows his business. There's your lady traveller, who's always handy with a penny piece and a pat on the head for a nice-spoke lad to clean her boots and hand her to her coach: and there's your old gentleman, maybe a bit careless with his purse, who doesn't know he dropped it till it's handed back, and then he's all gratitude and doesn't count his coins till it's too late: and there's mine host, who doesn't always think to lock his coffers, and your drunken traveller, snoring by the fire with purse wide open – oh, there's no lack of opportunity for a sharp-witted lad to keep his pocket lined. But the lining wasn't thick enough to suit my purpose. I'd a mind, as I've told you, friend, to take myself to London and set up as a gentleman in a style better suited to my tastes, and for that I needed money. I'd perceived long ago that it's not breeding alone provides a man with his station in life: that breeding's always cushioned with a fat fortune. And I reflected that if I could not have the one I might yet come by the other.

And so I turned all my energies to studying what might be done, and found myself remarkably well-placed for my ambitions. Indeed, before many months were out I had a diamond necklace thrown in my way, by the carelessness of a Lord What-Have-You and his Lady, washed up here by a summer storm. But the hue and cry was raised too soon, before I could make my escape, and I had to rid myself of the plunder and cry 'Thief!' with the rest. By good fortune I was able to shift suspicion on to a poor wretch called Tom – a half-witted thing that carries water and the like for my master, lank as a mongrel dog and quite weak in the head. The necklace was found in his mattress, where I'd put it, but Tom lost his job and wandered after that like a mindless ghost beyond the walls, to pick up what he could and fix me with a look as though his poor brain knew what had passed.

Thus foiled in my intentions, I became increasingly more gloomy and thought I'd never find another chance to seize, but once again good luck was on my side. This inn lies on the drove road from Wales, and we have much custom from the Welsh drovers conducting their business with the markets of Smithfield, Buckingham, Aylesbury and beyond. They bring droves and wethers and black Welsh cattle, many hundred at a time, and I fancy they must be sharper fellows than they appear, to undertake such journeys with success, matching themselves against the adversities of nature and bringing their beasts to the market at such a time and in such a condition as to ensure themselves of a fat profit. Indeed, it is widely held that many of these fellows are men of substance, though you'd scarce believe it to see them: a scurvy lot they are, rogues to a man, black-browed, wheedling creatures, as stunted as their scraggy beasts. Being long accustomed to them in this region, the farmers hereabouts do a good business in hiring out a piece for grazing to them when they make their stand for the night, while my master at the inn does a fair trade in slaking their thirsts, for they're insatiable brutes and drink themselves from one village ale-house to the next. Many's the time I've had to boot the sodden fellows from out my master's stable.

But I stray from my tale. For it was a pair of these drovers played into my hands and set the whole thing going, that ended in the woods tonight. They passed through here in June, bound for Smithfield with a great drove, as large as ever I've seen, and prime beasts at that, putting it into my mind as I saw them that there went a nice heavy bag of gold sovereigns on the hoof, as you might say. There were three fellows with them: two Welsh rogues, and an Englishman, one they call Big Sam, a cattle-dealer who's in partnership with the Welsh drovers and accompanies them on their journeys, paying their debts and the like. He rode ahead on this occasion to ask for lads in the village to help bring the drove through, as is often done, and I, thinking to earn a few pence, went out with the rest and chivvied for a while, till they were out of the village and on their way, when I collected my reward and made for home.

They say it takes a thief to catch a thief, and maybe by the same token it takes a rogue to smell out another. At any rate, no sooner did I spot two of the rascals, Big Sam and one of the Welshmen, crouched down behind a hedge, deep in talk, than my nose told me there was something afoot, and it would do me no harm to keep myself informed. So I crept along the ditch, as quiet as a fox stalking a rabbit, until I could hear what they said, and then I lay still, and what I heard gave me food for thought – a feast indeed, a whole Sunday dinner of it.

For they were planning murder, no less. It seemed that the two Welshmen had fallen out, and Big Sam had sought to turn the situation to his own advantage by fanning the flames of their disagreement. And now the pair of them, Big Sam and his henchman, a weasel-faced runt named Dewi, had it in mind to make away with number three, the big fellow they called Black Gwyn. The crime was to take place not then, but later, when the beasts were sold and the proceeds in their pockets, and they were turned for the journey back to their godforsaken valleys, to make payment for their stock to the Welsh farmers who bred them. But, and here was the merriest cut of all, they'd go back empty-handed, with a sorry tale of how they'd been set upon by highwaymen, by the notorious Driftway Jim, no less, and all their money taken, and their poor companion, their dear friend, shot dead by the thief and laid by them to rest in English soil ... The money, look you, would lie hid, safe in some hole or tree till they saw fit to come back and help themselves to what was not their own, and then I daresay their Welsh friends would not see them again for many a long year, till all was spent. Oh, a fine tale they made of it: why, I had tears in my eyes to hear them tell of how they wept over their friend's corpse, and how reverent they buried him, and how brave they fought to drive off the brute who killed him. For there they sat, all amid the sparkling may, and with the lark singing away as sweet as you like above their heads, and worked on their tale till they had it all to their satisfaction. And then up comes their poor doomed companion, who'd been rounding up stray beasts, and they bawl good cheer at him as merry as you please, and off they all go, down the Driftway with their sheep and their bullocks and the load of villainy in their hearts.

And leaving me, as I've said, with a pretty meal of information to chew over at my leisure, for, depend upon it, I'd not let a chance like this go slip. Here were two wretches, planning to make away with a goodly fortune (for I'd counted their herd, and saw there were over three hundred head), and with a crime on their hands to boot so that if I could but turn the tables on them they'd dare not squeal, lest their evil deed be found out. In the end, it was their talk of Driftway Jim gave me my plan. It's true enough he rides the Driftway, but he's not been seen in these parts for a while now, and they say he's moved his pitch over beyond Northampton, and takes his plunder on the heaths and moors some thirty miles away. Though like all gentlemen of the road he has a way of popping up in one place and then another so you'd think he must have wings at least. Well, I thought, and hugged myself with joy at my own cunning, at my own devilish craft, if they wanted Driftway Jim, then Driftway Jim they should have . . .

And now I had to keep my patience, and play the waiting game, for according to my reckoning, I must allow so many days for them to complete their journey to London and so many more for their return, before I should see them again. Never did time so drag his feet: I fretted and fumed and cursed each smiling day, thinking myself mocked by the cuckoo's song, and the nodding heads of roses blooming by the waysides.

At last they came, slinking into the inn for ale and food like a pair of mangy hounds. For a pair they were: there was neither sight nor sound of number three. I was beside myself with joy to see them come, and indeed they were quite perplexed to find themselves given such a welcome, for I made it my business to see they were well cared for, and drew their ale myself. I was sore tempted to ask tenderly for their good companion, whether he were well, and how the journey went for him, but held myself back in case they grew alarmed. For they were all of a twitch, glancing here and there from under those shaggy Welsh brows, clinging to one another like a pair of lovers, keeping aloof from their fellow travellers: oh, if ever I saw guilt, it was in that wretched pair. I stabled their horses for them – for they came mounted on a pair of rough Welsh ponies – and saw them bedded down in the outhouse beyond the yard, that's set aside for drovers. And then I made haste to the stables, for I had work to do.

I'd not been idle through those tedious days: I had a cloak, a fine lace shirt (taken from the effects of one Lord John Hope, who'd more than was good for him in that line), a peruke (that belonged to a gentleman who died upon the road: I bought it from his servant), a pair of boots I had to clean and somehow forgot to return to their owner. And, lastly but not least, my master's pistol.

I'd have dearly liked to see myself, thus attired, and masked to boot: for I felt a fine fellow, every inch the highwayman, Driftway Jim himself sprung suddenly to life, lurking there in the stable till all should be quiet and I could be safely on my way. For I had some miles to ride: there's a wood, to the west, a dismal place where no one goes, and there I planned to wait till morning, and surprise them as they passed, trusting they'd leave at dawn, as was their habit, and I could be back in Culworth, stripped of my disguise, before the day was old.

There was a full moon, ripe as a cream cheese, so I scarce needed the lantern I had slung from the saddle as I led my master's good brown mare from the stable and through the yard (her hooves bound with cloth to dull the sound). Like a wraith I moved, behind the snoring inn, and thought myself clear until I saw I had a companion, skulking against a cottage wall, a figure black in the moonlight, watching. I pulled up sharp, and my stomach did some pretty turns, I can tell you, until the creature moved his head and I saw it was none but poor idiot Tom, staring as though he'd seen the Devil himself, as well he might.

I swung up on the horse, and passed nearby him. He opened his mouth, and called me by my name (not mine, mark you, but that I'd borrowed with my clothes – Jim): I should have observed that he seemed more taken by surprise than fright, but I was too busy with my own concerns. Thinking to have some sport, though, I thrust down the kerchief round my mouth and pulled a face at him, knowing the poor fool could tell no tales, for there's none here pays him as much attention as a dog. And indeed, his jaw fell open at the sight and he turned and fled away into the night as though he had urgent business somewhere beyond the village, so that I rode on my way grinning at his discomfiture.

The moon rode with me, swinging above the trees like a private lamp, and I was in fine spirits, with my pistol on my hip, afraid of no one and thinking maybe here was an occupation worthy of my consideration, though I didn't fancy the chance of a promising career being cut off short on the gallows at Tyburn, as happens to such gentlemen from time to time. No, I thought, better to take the fortune so nearly in my grasp, and set up as a real gentleman, this side of the law. So I urged on my horse, and kicked her to quell her fancies, for she shied at the trees as though she saw substance in the shadows, and turned her head to neigh and snort, making believe we had company on the empty road.

Dawn found me waiting in the wood with the present of a fine white mist to serve me as a shroud, so that I might stay hid among the trees but near enough the track to fall upon my prey as soon as they should show themselves. The wood shifted and muttered to itself, as woods are wont to do, and I was hard put to it to convince myself I was alone, and my horse still more: but I fought off such foolish fancies, and concentrated my mind on the prize that lay ahead, until at last I heard the sound of hoof-beats on the road, and then I drew out my pistol, gathered up the reins, and held myself ready.

They came out of the gloom at a fast trot, riding one behind the other, and I was upon them in a flash, before they could bawl 'Thief', and had Big Sam staring down the barrel of my gun and quaking like a stupid hare fixed by a pointing dog. The other fellow would have made off until I had him covered too, and then they both set to whining and crying for mercy, which so inflamed me that I was tempted to blow their brains out, until I reflected that if they died their crime would die with them, which might prove inconvenient, and it were better for me to let them go. So I bellowed at them that if they valued their lives they'd better look to and find some payment for them, at which they cringed and fawned and made haste to pass me the bags of sovereigns they had hid beneath their garments. I made sure they'd given me all they had (and indeed the wretched Dewi had yet another stuffed beneath his saddle flap), and then curled my whip over their ponies' flanks, cocked my pistol at them and told them to be on their way, at which they made off down the track and out of sight as fast as rabbits down a hole.

I hitched the reins around my horse's neck, and sat myself down to contemplate my plunder. It was every bit as pretty as I'd thought: there's no finer sight, in my opinion, than the chink and glitter of a pile of coins. There's a texture, a variety, a fineness of design, that you'll not perceive in any of your masterpieces of Nature. Thus I reflected, digging my hands into the elegant heap, pouring the stuff from hand to hand. And then, all of a sudden, I heard the whisper of a step upon the fallen leaves, and leaped to my feet, to find myself confronted by a twin, a shadow, my very double, Driftway Jim himself.

My hand, flying to the pistol in my belt, was knocked aside by his with a crack that made me yelp. Another blow had me sprawling at his feet, begging for mercy, while his boot pounded my ribs and rolled me off my prize, which I had sought to cover with my body. Seeing the game was up, I implored him to take it all if only he would leave me be, for the fellow was toying with his pistol as though he were in two minds whether to try out his marksmanship, and my own (or rather, that I'd borrowed) was kicked beyond my reach among the trees.

'Why should I spare you?' says he. 'Presumptuous wretch.'

'Oh, sir,' I cried. 'Think of my poor widowed mother, whose sole support I am. It was for her I did it, I swear to you. I only wanted to buy comforts for her dying years,' and I set to bawling and weeping as loud as I could, for I've heard tell your gentleman of the road is often a soft-hearted fellow.

Looking up, to see if my words did aught to melt his heart, my eyes fell upon a figure beyond him, standing back among the trees, and at the sight I let out a screech of another kind. For I'll swear what I saw was an apparition, a phantom, the ghost of Black Gwyn, and as I shrieked it seemed to me he opened his mouth, and laughed aloud . . .

'Pah!' says Driftway Jim, hitching the bags of gold to his saddle, at which I wailed and shrieked the louder. 'I'll not waste good powder on such a wretch,' and with that he gives my mare a cut about the quarters with his whip that sends her scampering for home, and bawls at me to take myself off before he changed his mind, the which I did with all speed, feeling his boot endorse his words, and fled down the track, my ill-fated disguise all streaked in mud and dirt, into the light of a jeering dawn.

So there's my tale, friend, and a fine progression of infamy it is. I'm back where I began, with nothing to show for my ambitions but a sore head where the ostler clouted me for coming late to work today. I've lost my fortune, my master's lost his pistol, the Welsh rogues have lost their gold, and one of them his life, and the only one to gain from the whole ill-contrived affair is a highwayman. And poor half-witted Tom, who, I learn too late, has kept strange company this many a long day now, and who's not so addled in the brain he can't seize an opportunity to make merry andrews of us all.

The voice trailed away into a hoarse chuckle, and then that, too, grew softer and finally vanished, as though soaked up by the walls of the yard. Paul became aware once more of other sounds which seemed to have been in some way suspended during the telling of the story: the grinding noise of the dog chewing its bone, and the muffled talk and clatter from inside the pub. Sandra threw out an arm convulsively, sat up, and was suddenly wide awake. She looked at him and said, 'Why're you smiling like that, Paul?'

'Oh, just something. It doesn't matter.'

Old Bill came out of the pub, unhitched Bessie's reins, and swung himself up on to the cart.

'You'll be tired of waiting, I daresay. I met an old mate of mine. Get up there, Bess.'

'I didn't mind,' said Paul. 'There was another of those – messages. Not a sad one, this time. Shall I tell you?'

'You do that, son. Pass the time.'

They rumbled down the quiet village street, the lights in the windows glowing orange in the grey evening light. Paul retold Jack's story.

'I'm sorry,' he ended, apologetically, 'I can't make it funny the way he did. Funny even though there was a murder. He made it seem neat, like a circle – everybody getting what they deserved and nobody really being any the worse off.'

'Ah, but they were,' said Bill. 'What about those blokes back in Wales, who never got the money for their cows?'

'Oh. Yes. I'd forgotten about them. Yes, of course.'

'There you are, you see. Things don't happen in circles. It's more like dropping a stone into a pond: you make ripples and they bump into each other and make more ripples. Eh? And there's always more than one way of looking at things.'

'Yes. Yes, I see what you mean. The way he told that story, it was only the way it seemed to him. For any of the other people in it, it would have been quite different.'

'Aye. That's right. Or anything else for that matter. This ride we're making now, for example. I'll be bound it looks quite different to me than it does to you. Or the little 'un here.'

Paul looked at Sandra. She'd found a length of string somewhere in the debris that littered the bottom of the cart and was absorbed in twisting it round her fingers, trying to make a cat's cradle: she looked content and unruffled, clearly she'd quite forgotten the police, or even, perhaps, why they were there and where they were going. It was like that at home, often. Something would happen – just some little thing, it could be – and he'd get all worked up, his head bursting with feelings, so loud and strong it seemed as though anyone else within half a mile must be able to see or hear them too, and then Dad or Christine would start to talk, quite ordinary, about something quite different, and he'd realize they had no idea, didn't know at all ... It hadn't been the same for them, whatever it was hadn't happened in the same way. So it must be true the other way round, mustn't it? There must be things going on inside their heads he didn't know about.

Dad? He wasn't a great one for talking, Dad. Just sometimes. But that didn't mean he wasn't there, did it? 'He's been lonely,' Gran had said. He never said he was lonely. But he wouldn't, would he? It's not the sort of thing you go out and announce to people, is it? Gran knew, though. I never really thought about it.

Her. Christine. She talks quite a lot, really, stories about things she's seen and people she's known, that kind of thing. She makes Sandra laugh: not me, though. She doesn't get fussed easily, so it's hard to know what she's feeling, often, or thinking. Sometimes she goes quiet for a long time. She's always trying to talk to me: asking about school, and that.

And I don't ever answer. Just 'Yes' or 'No'. Not proper answers.

Paul stared at his fingernails: they were unattractive, dirty, and bitten right down. He thought they looked horrible. He thought that he felt like they looked. It wasn't a new feeling, either.

'What's up?' Bill was peering at him, sharp-eyed.

'Nothing.' He was flattened by gloom, defeated.

'Well,' said Bill. 'You are down in the dumps, aren't you? Cheer up, son. I daresay you're getting peckish. Tell you what, we'll call in on a friend of mine, just up the road here. Name of Sarah Slatter. She'll have a bite to spare, like as not. She's a good sort. I like to call in on her when I'm in these parts: give her a few bits and pieces I've picked up. It's hard for old folk, living on the pension.'

5

The cottage was some way from the village, isolated in the fields. They came upon it suddenly, or rather it came upon them, materializing out of the mist, agreeably solid in the dissolving landscape. It was small and very old, all the corners of the stone blunted by time, the slate roof sagging. In the small patch of garden beside it a regiment of cabbages marched away into obscurity.

Sarah Slatter was a small woman with a sharp face: she peered round the door at them like a rodent in a burrow, suspicious. Then she saw who it was.

'Bill! I've not got my glasses on, I couldn't see you, with the fog come down so. Come on in. I'll put the kettle on.'

'I've got company, Sarah. Pair of kids.'

The old woman fished in her pocket for a pair of steel-rimmed spectacles. 'There, that's better. Why, so you have. Bring them in, then.'

The front door opened straight into a small, cluttered room. A wooden table and chairs, a battered armchair leaking stuffing, a bright, worn rug in front of the fireplace, a dresser crammed with oddments – china, old framed photographs, a loudly ticking clock. An old brown wireless played music softly, with much crackling. There was a smell of cooking.

Bill put a bundle down on the table. 'Some bits and pieces, Sarah. Might be some use to you. There's a good coat, and a blanket. You get a lot of good stuff put out as scrap, some of these big houses I call at.'

66

'Thank you kindly. I'll not say no.' She patted Bill on the arm, then moved round and patted the children: it was as though words were not enough, to make real contact she must touch as well. Paul saw Sandra flinch, and felt angry with her: you couldn't hurt her feelings, not someone old like that. Fortunately the old woman didn't seem to notice: she was asking Sandra her name.

'Would you like some bread and dripping, dear?'

'Yes, please,' said Paul, nudging Sandra, who still stared.

Bill said he had to see to the animals, and went out into the twilight. Sarah made the children sit down, and began to get out cups and a loaf of bread. The wireless erupted suddenly into a fit of crackling and spluttering. She fiddled with the knobs, tutting irritably.

'Awkward thing! You never know where you are with it. It's old, see. My daughter give it to me, years ago. My daughter that married an Oxford man. But I like to have it. It's company, being as I'm on my own now.'

Through the atmospherics there came the time-signal, and then a man reading the news. Paul looked round the room: there was a glass case with a stuffed bird in it, and some medals, tarnished and with faded ribbons, framed in another case beside it.

The old woman said, 'That's my husband's medals. My Sam. He got them in France, in the first war. He were gone four years. Four years. And it were the only time he ever left Culworth, in all his life. All that way, to fight in the mud. Thousands and thousands of them. And then back here, to be a cowman for another forty year. I don't know.' She sighed, staring at the medals. Paul couldn't think of anything to say.

'Here. Here's his picture. That's when we were married. He were a good-looking chap, eh?'

The photograph was brown with age: it was a studio

portrait, showing a young Sarah, a bride, clutching a young man's arm, the two of them framed in white mist, as though they stood in a cloud.

'That was a long time ago. You begin to forget things, when you get old. I like to have that by me, to remember, like.'

Paul said, 'What's the other picture?'

The photograph was in a double frame. On the other side was another fading print: two old people, man and woman, the woman in a dress to her ankles, the man in some odd garment, almost like a dress. They stood in front of the cottage.

'That's my Sam's great-grandmother, that is. And her husband. I can remember her when I was a girl: they lived in this cottage, see, and I lived over the hill. Old Nelly, they used to call her. Full of stories she was. I remember she used to tell us children that when she were a child her mum used to scare her by telling her that if she was naughty Bonaparte would come and get her. There, you're looking at a picture of a person who was alive when Napoleon Bonaparte was alive. Fancy that, eh?'

'What is it he's wearing, the white thing?'

'That's a smock.' She chuckled. 'That's what country folk wore, in those days. A lady come once, buying old things, and I sold her my dad's. She give me more for it than it cost new. A thing he'd worn for working. And her in a big shiny car. I had to laugh.' She moved over to the wireless and turned the sound up. 'I want to hear the weather. I'll need to cover my potatoes if there's a frost.'

'... the fog now dense in some parts of the Midlands should clear before dawn giving way to rain spreading from the west. There is a possibility of frost in low-lying areas. And now here's Tom Barnett with the local news ... The dispute at B.M.C.'s Cowley depot was settled tonight and three hundred workers on the Mini assembly line are expected to go back to work on Monday. The Minister of Housing, speaking in Birmingham today, said that the present government's record on housing and slum-clearance was better than that of any government since the war. On the B4525 between Banbury and Northampton police patrols stopped cars this afternoon and set up road-blocks in their hunt for two ...'

Sarah switched off the wireless. 'There. That's enough of that.'

Paul started forward. 'Oh, please, no. I ...'

'Eh? What's that?'

'Nothing. It doesn't matter.'

His stomach was churning again. The bread and dripping, which Sandra was eating with relish, suddenly tasted horrible and he pushed the plate to one side. Two what? Two escaped prisoners? Two bank robbers? Or two children caught shoplifting who ran away from the police?

Not *caught* shoplifting. *Accused* of shoplifting.

Same thing, isn't it? As far as they're concerned.

Old Bill came in, with a rush of cold air, his hair glistening with beads of damp.

'Nasty night. We won't be stopping long. These two want to get to Cold Higham, and we can't have 'em on the road all night, eh?'

'But you'll have a cup of tea?' Sarah was already pouring tea into thick china cups.

'You know I never say no to a cup of tea.'

Paul, stirring his, thought: we're always drinking tea, on this journey, and I don't even like it. The cottage was very quiet, except for Sarah and Old Bill chuckling at each other over some private joke, the kettle hissing on the stove, the clock ticking. The noise of a car on the road outside made him stiffen and watch the door until it was safely past. They were all right in here, he supposed. But out there ... And they'd have to go, sooner or later. He looked at the clock. Twenty-five to seven. If he was at home, he'd be having tea. Dad would just be getting back from work. What a row that clock made: tick, tick, tick. Like rain tapping on the window, or someone hammering, with a very small hammer ... It was getting darker and darker in the cottage, and cold. Funny, had that candle been on the dresser all the time? He hadn't noticed it before. And that round black pot hanging over the fire from a hook in the beam above the fireplace. And why was Sarah suddenly standing at the table, looking at the door like that? Except that it wasn't Sarah, was it, but someone else, younger, dressed differently? And why on earth was she holding a dead hare?

The woman said, 'Quiet, Sam. There's someone outside.'

The ticking stopped. There was a man in one corner of the room, sitting on a wooden stool, with a leather boot turned sole upwards between his knees, a small hammer in his hand, a couple of nails tucked between his lips. He, too, stared towards the door: their faces were grave with anxiety, the man and the woman. Into the silence came the crunch of feet somewhere beyond the door, and in the dark square of the curtainless window a light bobbed.

The man said very quietly, 'It's gamekeeper all right. Get it away, Nelly.'

The woman opened a wooden chest against the wall, pushed the hare inside, looked round wildly, picked up a blanket from a child's cot by the fireplace, put that on top, closed the lid. There was a knock at the door: the woman was wiping a bloodstain from her hand.

70

The door opened. A man with a lantern stood there. He shone the lantern into the bare room, on to the staring, sullen faces: the man, the woman, two children crouched by a brushwood fire.

'Sam Slatter?'

'Aye. That's me.'

'You been out tonight?'

'I have not.'

'There's mud on your boots.'

'I been up the road to draw water from the well.'

Silence, breathing. Eyes, staring. Suddenly the man with the lantern walked over to the black pot on the fire, lifted the lid, sniffed.

The woman said, 'Potatoes and cabbage water. Like every night.' She said it savagely, in a hard, angry voice.

The man with the lantern held it up, sent yellow light into the dark corners, on to the dresser, the scrubbed table, the two chairs, the bare stone floor.

'There was poachers up in Lord Mansfield's woods tonight. They been seen. It'll be jail when we find out who it were.'

Silence. Breathing. The children still, except for eyes following the man with the lantern.

He went to the door, opened it. Went out.

The man took a nail from his mouth, held it against the sole of the boot, began to tap. Tick, tick, tick. The woman sat down at the table, stiff-backed, wooden-faced, listening to the footsteps going away. Then suddenly she flopped forward, her head on her arms, shoulders heaving. Laughing? Crying?

The man said, 'Give over, Nelly. He's gone.' He got up, went to the fire, stirred it and made sparks fly up. 'There. Let's have a bite to eat, eh, Nelly?'

*

Old Bill's voice made Paul start. 'I said we'd best be getting on, now you've had a bite to eat. Eh, son?'

He looked at the clock. Twenty-five to seven. Tick, tick, tick.

It hadn't stopped. Something else must have done. Like dreams, when you're half-awake, in the early morning, seeming to go on for ages when that wasn't possible.

He said, 'The great-grandmother you talked about, the one in the photograph – was her husband called Sam?'

'That's right. All the men in my husband's family were called Sam.'

'I see.' He looked at the corner. A three-legged stool, with a man mending his own boots. Now there was a little table with a white lace cloth on it, another framed photograph, of two children, and a vase inscribed 'A Present from Brighton'.

Sandra, who'd been very silent, said, 'Thank you for my tea,' and then yawned, hugely.

'You're welcome, my love,' said Sarah.

'Cheerio, then, Sarah.'

'Cheerio, Bill.'

'Good-night,' said Paul. 'Thank you very much.' He looked round the room once more: it was warm, friendly.

'Good-night, my dear.'

Outside, Bessie stood slumped between the shafts, head down, her muscles slack beneath the skin as though she might fall apart at a touch: hearing them, she laid back one ear, lifted a hoof, and came together again, rolling the whites of her eyes.

'Hey, up!' said Bill. 'Work for you, my girl.' The donkeys were grazing on the verge, stiff-legged as toys. 'Hitch 'em up for me, son.'

They were on their way again, rolling forward into the

muffled world that forever retreated before them. Sandra said unexpectedly, 'That was a nice lady. She was like our Gran.'

'I've been calling in on Sarah for ten years or more. Since I took to the road, I reckon.'

'Did you live somewhere once, then?' said Paul, surprised.

'I did. Most of my life. Though I won't say it suited me: I were always restless. I'd take off from time to time even then. My wife would get very put out, poor soul. But I always found it difficult to keep my mind on the same things as other people: making money, and getting on in the world, and that. It didn't seem to me that important.' He took the pipe out of his pocket, lit it, sucked appreciatively, and sent a cloud of smoke rolling into the mist. 'Doesn't bother you, does it, son? It's a right strong smell, I know that. I like a heavy tobacco.'

'I don't mind a bit,' said Paul. 'Did you live in an ordinary house, then, all full of things, like other people?'

'Oh, I had things, yes. Roomfuls of 'em. It got so all my time was spent looking after these things, getting more. And then my wife died, and I looked at all these things, and I thought: Well, blow that. What's the use of all this stuff to me? I can't talk to it, nor's it going to keep me warm at night. So I got rid of the lot. The neighbours thought I'd gone off my rocker, I can tell you.' He chuckled, 'Maybe I had, to their way of thinking. I didn't keep a thing, except the clothes on my back, and a bit of money to buy the cart and the animals. I'm a healthy man, I always liked to be in the open air, and I wanted to be my own master for the time that was left me, not being beholden to anyone, not doing anything I didn't have the inclination for. I've not regretted it, nor anything I left behind.'

'Aren't you cold in the winter?'

'Not so bad I can't stand it. I've been colder doing things I hadn't the stomach for, day in, day out, just to be like other folk. Cold in the mind, see?'

All at once there was a splitting, breaking noise. Bill pulled suddenly on the reins: Bessie threw up her head and lurched to a halt with an exaggerated stagger of protest. The children were flung forward and clung to each other to keep from falling off the cart.

'Drat it!' said Bill. 'It's that rotten shaft gone again. We'll have to pull in and do some repair work.' He looked up and down the road: it was narrower here, without the wide grass verges, and from time to time cars swished past them, sliding out of the mist with fiery headlights. 'We'll have to go a bit farther – I know a place we can stop.'

Round the next bend the mist thinned out, standing back to reveal an island of dusk with only a faint suggestion of milkiness in the air to remind them of what they had left. In the midst of it stood a house, neatly curtained against the night, set in grass shorn close as a cat's fur. Paint gleamed on the front door; trapped flowers stood motionless in squares and crescents; a fence of looped chain kept the world at bay. Old Bill drove the cart off the road on to the grass in front of it. 'This'll do. We'll not take long. Get my bag of tools from the back, son.'

'This?'

'That's right. Now, you hold these nails, see, and hand me one every time I yell out.'

They worked in silence. Sandra slid down from the cart and wandered off to investigate the hedgerows.

'It's a proper botched-up job, this,' said Bill. 'But it'll have to do till I can get myself a new shaft. There's a mate of mine runs a timber-yard in Northampton: I'll have to look in on him.'

In the front of the house, a curtain twitched, showing

a sliver of light. 'There's someone watching us,' said Paul.

'I don't doubt there is. They're "keep out" kind of folk round here, these new houses. I know this place. I bought a bit of scrap here – old sink – last time I was in these parts, and the lady asked me if I'd do some work for her. Jobbing gardener kind of stuff. But I didn't fancy it, not just then, so I said no, and she was quite put out.'

The front door opened. Two people came out, man and woman, middle-aged. They advanced down the path. Half-way, the woman stopped and said, 'It is the same man. I thought so. That old tramp. We can't have him dumping himself down here right in front of the house. All that clutter. So unsightly. Besides, I don't like the idea of . . .' her voice became inaudible, though only just.

The man said, 'I'll deal with him, dear. You go inside.' Paul stared as he strode towards them: short, plump, his skull shining pink in the middle of a horse-shoe of thin hair, clean, smelling of bathrooms and polish.

'Here,' he said, 'you. I can't have this. You can't put yourself down here. Move along, will you.'

'Right you are,' said Bill amiably. 'Just a tick while we get this fixed up, and we'll be off.' He stooped over the cart again, hammering. The man stared, anger seeming to grow in him as he watched.

'Damn great wheelmarks,' he said. 'Right in front of my property. Are you going or aren't you?'

Bill grunted something, intent on what he was doing.

Suddenly the man erupted into rage. 'Now! You get going now. See? Otherwise I'm getting on to the police. They know what to do with people like you – layabouts, sponging off honest people . . . Go on, get moving, or do I call the police?'

Police! Paul's mounting indignation suddenly crumbled

away into alarm. He grabbed Bill's arm and whispered, 'Come on! Let's go. Please.'

'All right, son, all right. Don't let him get you fussed – the pesky little fellow.' He finished what he was doing, refusing to be hurried, stowed away the tools, called Sandra, tucked her into her sacks again, clicked his tongue at Bessie, all without once looking at the man, who stood staring as they rumbled away down the road.

'Beast!' said Paul, trembling. 'Horrible, horrible beast. How could he talk to you like that?'

'Easy. He reckoned he was better than what I am, one way and another, so it came easy. Better because he's got more things: he'd be a man that would set a lot of store by things. And he was bothered, too. People don't like someone who's different from them: rock-bottom different, that is. It's like they'd been criticized, you see, isn't it?'

'All the same, he'd got no right.'

'Ah, rights. Rights is funny things. There's no accounting for rights.'

'Will he call the police, do you think?'

Bill shrugged. 'Maybe. Maybe not. What's it to us?'

A car swam out of the mist, goggle-eyed, passed them, and disappeared: Paul moved his head round slowly to watch it go. Police cars have those flashing blue things on top, don't they? You'd see that at once: or are there times when they don't use them? When they're trying to take people by surprise, for instance?

Sandra said, 'Is it the night-time?'

'Nearly.' Bill shook the reins. 'Get up there, old girl! We'll have to push on a bit, if you want a roof over your heads tonight.' Bessie heaved herself reluctantly into a trot, and settled into the rhythm of it, the cart rocking and swaying. The movement was soothing: Paul leaned against the heap of unidentifiable objects behind him, Sandra slumped against his side, and closed his eyes. The cart creaked like a ship riding the wind, Bessie's feet hit the tarmac with a regular, solid beat: there were no other sounds, except the gentle patter of the donkeys and faint snuffling noises from the sleeping Sandra. He travelled backwards in his mind, to the house, his room, the kitchen, Dad, Christine. What were they doing? I don't think we should have done this. Just gone off, without saying. I mean me, not we – it isn't Sandra's fault. She just does what I say. I should have gone back – said, 'I'm going off to Gran's, and that's it.' But I couldn't, could I? Not with that policewoman after me. I had to, didn't I? All the same ...

He shifted uncomfortably, and sent his thoughts in the other direction, forward, to Gran's house. I wish we were there. We'll be all right there. Gran'll sort it out with Dad, and I'll say I'm sorry. I really will. But we've got to get there before the police find us. Otherwise ...

Tiredness crept through him, welcome, dulling his anxiety. He fell asleep, cradled by the movement of the cart.

When he woke there were readjustments to be made: things had changed. The darkness now was a real darkness, not just daylight muted by the fog: beyond the shifting curtain of white the sky was blue-black, arching in a circle above, before and behind. Bill had set a red lantern at the back of the cart, and another hung at the front: the two of them sent quivering shafts of light into the darkness, blunted and dispersed by the fog. And there was something else. Bessie's hooves no longer smacked down hard on tarmac, but thumped dully on grass.

Paul said sharply, 'Why aren't we on the road any more?'

'We are.'

77

'But it's grass.'

'It's not us left the road. It's the road left us. This is still the Driftway, but it's a green lane here, like it was in old times.'

'Oh, I see.'

A green lane, running between fields. No road, therefore no cars, therefore no police. A wonderful feeling of peace, of freedom, filled him. He stretched his legs, looked at Sandra, still sleeping, and peered into the enveloping dark. Hedges rode high on either side of them, their leaves reflecting an orange and red glow in the lantern light. The cart lurched and bumped on the rough track, responding to every irregularity of the ground, now running free on a stretch of grass, now dragged back as the wheels caught in a patch of mud. Bessie plodded with her ears irritably flattened, the picture of discontent.

'She reckons it's time we put up for the night,' said Bill. 'She don't go much for overtime, old Bess. But we got to get you to your Gran's, eh?'

'Thank you,' said Paul humbly.

'That's all right, son. To tell the truth, I'm partial to some company on the road now and again. I won't say I'm lonely, but I don't say no to a bit of a chat from time to time. And there's not so many fancy a lift on a cart nowadays.' He chuckled.

'Hitch-hikers?' said Paul.

Bill snorted. 'Them with rucksacks and fiddles? Girls in trousers? Not them. It's speed they're after. Here today and gone tomorrow. See how far you can get in a week. They're not real travellers, they're not. Real travelling's crawling your way over the country like a fly on a wall, hedge by hedge and hill by hill and village by village. From river to river and town to town. That way you feel the bones of the place, see? You see the way the land goes, and why they grow corn here and why they graze cattle there, and why there's cities where there are, and why there's a lot of people in one place and not so many in another. You see the way the shape of a country's made the people in it, and you see the way they've written themselves all over it, too, people who're dead and gone now. In the way the fields go, and the roads, and the things they've built, and the bits they've dug up or cut down or flooded or drained or not been able to find a use for at all.'

There was a silence. Bill seemed sunk in thought, his sharp eyes staring over Bessie's back into the darkness.

'Go on.'

'Eh?'

'Please go on. About the country, and people making it, and all that.'

'Ah. It's a bit of a hobby-horse of mine, that. Most people look at a bit of country and they just see it as an arrangement of hedges, and trees, and lanes, and they don't think of how it's all come about, like. They think it's natural. There's hardly such a thing as a natural landscape. It's something that's always on the move, changing every few years. And if you get to know a bit about it you can see all the layers of changes, going right back into old times: where there's been a village that's gone now, or a road that's got forgotten, like this one, or a quarry that's grassed over now but once spewed out enough stone to build a town. And the way towns have grown up, and then maybe died a little because the river they were built on got less important when the railways came, or because the things people made there weren't needed any more when something else came along to take their place. And the way when people began to be more than just farmers they had to go where there's water and rock: water to drive mills and rock to burrow into for coal. It's been a long business, getting hold of a place and learning how to use it: a long, hard business.'

'And now there's nothing left of what it was to begin with,' said Paul. 'Moors and forests and all that.'

'Just here and there. Old places, from right back.'

Paul looked out into the darkness. The silence concealed the landscape he knew: the neat, orderly landscape of hedgerows, shapely trees, hills lifted to meet sky and cloud, fields, streams, squat cottages, a landscape that seemed set and unchanging in all but the variety of season, the variety of colour and of light. But it was not. Beneath it lay all these other things: people working, fighting, dying. The fog rolled back before the cart, revealing a tree, a twist in the track, a clump of cow-parsley heads splayed against the hedge: he imagined other eyes in other times looking at the same things, feeling the same feelings, thinking . . . No, not thinking the same things. That would be the difference.

'You can't know how they thought,' he said. 'Not really.'

'I s'pose not, son. But we should try. We should do that.'

The cart lurched and bumped over the rough ground. This was a different kind of movement, not at all like the smoothness of the road. Paul thought that it must be more like travelling had always been along here. You could feel the contours of the land, the slant of the cart as it went uphill, the twist as the track took a turn to left or right.

Bill said, 'There's an old camp somewhere hereabouts.' He gestured vaguely into the darkness with his whip. 'I don't rightly remember where. Maybe we've passed it.'

'Camp? An army camp, you mean? From the war?'

'No. Nothing like that. It's what they call places where there's been people living a long way back. Where there's nothing left now. Just a green mound. That's what this one is, a green hill.'

Paul stared round. If there was any such thing here it was hidden now by darkness and fog.

'From prehistoric times, they are,' said Bill, 'when this place was empty. Just a few people strung out here and there. Tribes, and that. And the road. Parts of it are from that far back, I've heard.'

Empty. Paul tried to imagine this landscape empty, bared, stripped of all those things Bill had talked about, all the marks made on it by people over hundreds and hundreds of years, and left as it had been in the first place – hostile, unpredictable, unknown, reaching away into infinity, with people existing as it were by courtesy of forest, river and hill. People who were isolated, precarious, and not yet able to stamp themselves upon this place that would determine all they did: afraid of it, and dependent upon it. Images flickered in his head: a green mound, the road as a track reaching away and away, people so different as to be unimaginable ... But still people, like me, or Bill.

Islands of people in a harsh world, pushing back the ferocity of the wilderness just enough to use what there was to be used, to begin to put down roots, to explore the whole complex business of living with one another. And for that, the road would be the very lifeline, the artery along which everything must come: war and peace, hope and fear, trade and change.

A dog barked somewhere to the right, a long way away. They must be following the rim of a valley, for the sound defined a distance, coming from below and quite far, clear and undistorted. The rhythm of Bessie's trot changed imperceptibly in response, and then levelled out again, as though it had told her something. Paul found himself stiffening a little in sympathy, trying to read the sound, invest it with significance, as though he was stirred by a memory of a time when the signals people lived by were different, simpler and yet more intense, the senses more acute, the store of knowledge small and immediately related to the business of survival, when every message must be sifted, considered, for it might be crucial . . .

6

The boy stopped. He listened, quite still, his head turned
a little towards the noise which had already ceased. It had
been a wolf: just one, not hunting, probably calling its
mate, far, perhaps an hour's journey across the valley
through the forest. The information received, assessed, he
moved on again, satisfied, and the dog at his heel moved
with him, nose to the ground, darting sometimes into the
coarse scrub at either side of the track. They moved at the
same even pace, boy and dog, a travelling pace, unhurried,
regular, surefooted over the rough ground, making no con-
cessions to weariness. For they had come far, to the very
limits of what was familiar, to the point beyond which the
tribe did not go, beyond which the word was unknown, the
shape of the land unfamiliar: after the next rise, the boy
knew, there would be a line of hills whose contours were
strange, and although the track went on, he would stop
there, observe what he had to observe, and then turn back
for the long return journey to the settlement.

The dog halted, stared into the density of trees above the
track, and the dark ridge of hairs lifting along its spine told
the boy that there were deer in there. It whined, and he
snarled at it: there was to be no hunting on this journey. He
could hear the deer himself, moving farther into the forest,
many of them from the sound: there was something dead,
too, not far off, a bear's kill maybe, with ravens on it, their
croaking muffled by the trees. This knowledge, too, he
stored, and the fact that below, in the valley, there was the
noise of water running full and busy: there had been rain.

The trees were thinning all the time, giving way to open scrubland: the track became a diffusion of small paths running wide across the turf. The boy made a swooping detour to avoid the place where once, long ago, before his time, but preserved in the memory of the people, two men from the tribe had been killed by strangers: as he did so his whole body twitched with anxiety, and he muttered to himself. As soon as he was past the place he forgot it, preoccupied again with smells and sounds, and a sudden hunger gnawing his belly. Once he stopped dead to investigate wolf droppings in the grass, but they were not fresh and he moved on again quickly: he was uncertain now, his tension betraying itself with an occasional stumble, though the ground here was smoother than farther back below the treeline, where the path was deeply rutted, littered with roots and fallen branches. Here, he was almost at the limits of his world: to known fears would soon be added unknown ones. The concealed threats of a place whose very outline was strange. But he need not venture into it. His task was a limited one: to travel the road, to this point and no further, to search for any sign of strangers, here or beyond, and report back to the settlement before sundown. In this way did the tribe protect itself against the danger of sudden attack.

He reached the top of the rise. Now the place beyond was wide open to him, fold upon fold of blue forest reaching away for ever under the grey sky, on and on. Behind him, the arrangement of hill, tree and valley was known, significant: in front of him, it was not. He observed it with the suspicion of a cat confronted by water, examining smells and sounds, noting the white glitter of a river among the trees, the long green humps of open ground on the hilltops, the darker colouring here and there that spoke of marshland, the differences of textures that told whether the forest was oak, beech or spruce.

And then he saw it, just below him, trickling up from the trees at the foot of the hill: a thread of blue smoke. The wind changed, and he smelt it too. He became agitated, running to and fro across the grass to get a better view of it, his hand on the knife at his waist. It told him something, but not enough. It told him there were men there, strangers, but not how many, or of what kind. One man, hunting? A war-party? It was not far away, just below him where the land tucked down again into the forest, right by the track: not far, but too far. He would be carrying out his task quite adequately if he returned to the tribe with just this fragment of information, but into his mind had come the idea that he could, perhaps should, go farther, creep down the hill and find out just who and what these strangers were. He was faced with a choice: unnerved by his indecision. He could defend himself alone against a wild beast, move confidently in the places he knew, but in a matter of this kind, involving other men, he needed the support of the tribe. He stood alone on the hilltop, under the wide sky, and the dog squatted patiently on its haunches, and watched him torment himself.

At last he decided. One moment he was standing there: the next he was trotting down the track, vanishing with it into the twilight world of the forest. But he moved now with extra care, almost without sound, his feet avoiding dead branches and twigs as though they saw them, seeking patches of grass and earth, his body passing from the shadow of one tree to that of another. He held his knife in his hand, and paused every few seconds to listen, and stare into the trees.

He smelt the strangers before he reached the clearing: they had cooked meat over a fire of larch twigs. The dog was growling in its throat, and he had to pull at the skin of its neck to quiet it. They moved through the last curtain of undergrowth together, as silently as two patches of mist, though the boy's stomach was doing the melting thing worse than he had ever known, worse even than the time he passed the black mouth of a cave and heard a bear roar inside.

The clearing opened before him, and there was the fire, ringed with black earth, and there beside it was the stranger, just one, stretched on some skins so that at first the boy thought he was dead. But then he saw him quiver and knew he was asleep. He wondered at such foolishness, and then saw that it was the sleep of fever: the stranger's skin was flushed and beaded with sweat, clearly he was sick. The boy's hand, clutching his knife, relaxed a little.

He examined everything, minutely, without moving a muscle: the skins on which the stranger lay, the animal bones heaped beyond the fire, the cooking-pot, the man himself, well-built, not old, his head turned away so that the boy could not see his features. Was he a hunter? There was a knife at his waist, and a spear stuck in the ground nearby. The sleeper threw out an arm in a convulsive gesture and knocked aside the skins, revealing a heap of knives, spearheads, axes. The boy understood at once: this was a trader, bound no doubt for the settlement, where he would barter his goods for the tribe's skins, dogs, or anything they had to offer. The knives and spearheads were good, he could see that even from where he stood: skilfully worked and well-balanced. The tribe would want them.

He decided to kill the stranger. He would achieve much honour with the older men of the tribe by returning with such a fine store of weapons, acquired without cost. The stranger, had he reached the settlement, would have been treated with the respect due to such a man, come in peace: the tribe did not kill in their own place unless they had to. But out here, in the strange part, he need feel no such obligations. Besides, the man was sick, and might never reach the settlement, and the weapons were very good.

The boy ran a finger lightly along the blade of his own knife: he selected the exact groove between the stranger's ribs that he would use, and moved forward.

A little wind stirred the ash of the fire, drifting it over the stranger's outstretched arms. He moved again, and turned his head towards the boy, so that for the first time he saw his face.

The boy had seen strangers before: twice. One had been another such trader: the others had been from another tribe, and they were dead. On both occasions he had been stunned – thrown into confusion by the sight of a human face that was not known to him. For all his life he had been surrounded by his own people: each one of them familiar. And now again he was amazed, looking down at features that were alien, and yet a mirror of his own. It was as though he recognized himself in the surface of a pool.

The man did not open his eyes. The boy stared at him: confused thoughts chased each other round his head: and out of them came the knowledge, simply, that he was not, after all, going to kill the stranger. The old, accustomed things said to him: this is a stranger, and therefore he is of no concern. Something new, disturbing, inscrutable, said: he is the same as I, we are of one kind.

He let the hand holding the knife fall to his side again. The stranger muttered in his sleep: the boy thought it likely that he would recover. He had seen this kind of sleep before in those coming from a fever, and his skin was damp, not dry and hot. The fire was smouldering sullenly: the boy stooped and banked the turf round it to keep it from going out. He touched one of the spearheads, considered whether he should take it, and thought that when the stranger recovered he would bring them to the settlement in any case. He would return now, and tell the tribe what he had seen, but he would say he had seen it from the hilltop, not from here. The tribe might wonder why he had not killed the stranger, and he had no words for the business of the two ideas that had fought each other in his head.

He turned, and melted again into the forest, hurrying because he was uneasy in this foreign place. He went up the hill too fast, at an awkward pace that brought him once or twice to his knees, but as soon as he reached the top he relaxed and fell again into the easy, travelling jog he had used before: he was with known things again, able to relate himself to his surroundings, contain the dangers that threatened. He pushed the matter of the stranger into a far corner of his mind, where it gnawed uncomfortably as a thing not understood: later, he might re-examine it, try to fit it into his store of accepted knowledge and predictable responses. Now, he allowed the feelings he knew to take over once more: caution, reassurance at the sight of a familiar tree or twist in the track, hunger, as a rabbit's scut bobbed in the bushes, waves of fear, and over everything, a deep need for the settlement, and the people. The light was getting thin: with his precise instinct for distance and the length of a day he knew that he would just get back before nightfall. He homed on the settlement, drawn towards it through the empty landscape: a lonely, purposeful figure in an endless and chaotic world.

Sandra was saying, 'Stop kicking me.'

'What?' He came awake with a start.

'You're kicking me. Your feet keep walking about in the air. What's the matter?'

'Nothing. I must've had a dream.'

'About playing football?'

'No,' he said irritably, 'about walking. Along this road.'

'My,' said Bill. 'You're proper taken up with this road, aren't you?'

He wanted to say, 'No, not by the road. By the people, not the road.' But that would just start Sandra off, asking a whole lot of questions. He stayed silent, thinking he'd dreamt himself into someone else's head, somehow: known, indistinctly, confusedly, what it had been like for this boy. And whatever it *had* been like, there was one thing that was the same. Just one. Other people. The business of other people.

He shook himself, and switched his attention back to now. 'Where are we?'

'Getting on,' said Bill. 'This is where we go back on the road again for a while. Just as well too. That shaft's taken a bit of a pounding along here: I don't like the noise it's making.'

Paul listened. 'It sounds as if it's going to bust again,' he said uneasily.

'I know. I'm not happy about it, to tell the truth.'

'Won't we be able to go on?'

'Maybe we'd better find you a lift. Stop a car or something, eh?'

'No,' said Paul violently. 'Please not. Let us stay with you. Please.'

Bill half-turned his head. 'Get you there quicker. It's turning out a nasty night.' It was too dark to see the old man's face: his voice sounded as though he might be smiling.

Paul said again, 'Please.'

'Oh, well. If you feel that badly about it we'd better do something about the old shaft, I suppose.'

Paul breathed again. 'What will you do?'

'There's a fellow I know who runs a pub just up here – we'll stop by and ask if he can let us have a bit of wood.'

They had come to a road again. The green lane they had been following joined it at a corner, so that though the road curved in from the left it was easy to see that the new road, and not the old, was the deviation. The headlights of cars wavered in the distance, and Paul's uneasiness came creeping back.

'I wish we were still on that old road. I liked it.'

Bill grunted. They could see the pub now: all lit-up and floating in the mist like a ship at sea. Bill steered Bessie into the car park which flanked it at the side, and then round to a backyard behind.

'Back entrance for us,' he said. 'Reckon we look a bit out of keeping with them Jaguars and Rovers. Might lower the tone of the place.' He chuckled. 'D'you want to come in with me, son?'

Paul hesitated.

'I do,' said Sandra. She was already sliding down from the cart, and he had to follow her, reluctant. He didn't want to get mixed up with people in a place like this, asking questions and that.

They went through a door into the back parts of the pub, full of barrels and boxes. A woman came out of a scullery wiping her hands on a cloth.

'Good gracious, you gave me a start! It's a long time since we set eyes on you, Bill. How are things with you?' She was looking curiously at the children.

'Fair enough. Fair enough. Is your old man around?'

'Here he is. Can you spare a moment, Sid?'

The man who had come through from the bar matched his wife: middle-aged, with a ready smile and a flow of talk. Bill explained his requirements. 'Sure. Sure. I can fix you up with something. We'll go out and have a look in my shed, Bill.' He spotted Paul, lurking uneasily by the door and said, 'Hello, hello. Who's this, then?'

'Young fellow I'm giving a lift to,' said Bill. 'Him and his little 'un.'

Paul could feel the woman's curiosity envelop him: friendly, but, under the circumstances, not welcome. He shuffled unhappily as the inevitable questions came.

'Isn't it a bit late for you to be out like this, dear? How old's your sister? Look at her, Sid, the little mite – you know she reminds me of someone, I just can't think for the moment ... Where did you say you were taking them, Bill? Do your parents know where you are, love? Couldn't we ring up your Gran, in case she's getting worried?'

'She hasn't got a telephone,' Paul mumbled, the last of a string of unwilling answers. He could feel Sandra staring at him: he'd said some things that weren't true, or that lay only on the edges of truth, and it was making him uncomfortable. She was too nice to tell lies to, this woman. For two pins he'd tell her all about it. Bill and the pub-owner had disappeared into the yard.

'Well, I don't know, I'm sure. I don't like the idea of children getting lifts on the road, I don't really.'

'We're all right. Honestly. Bill's been very kind.'

'Oh, I'm not worried about Bill. He's the salt of the earth, old Bill. I mean, just because he's a bit different from the rest of us in the way he likes to live doesn't mean he's any the worse, does it? No, it's your parents I'm worried for, dear.'

'We'll be there soon.'

'How much further did you say? Cold Higham? Couldn't I get someone to give you a lift in a car, dear? It would be ever so much quicker.'

'No, please ...' Paul began, but Bill, passing the door with a bag of tools in his hand, cut in.

'Don't you worry about 'em, Mrs Larkins. I'll deliver 'em safe and sound. We've got used to each other by now, as you might say. Tell you what, why don't you take them into the warm for a minute or two while I get going on this shaft of mine?'

The woman brightened. 'Right you are, Bill. Come along to the kitchen, then, my loves.'

They followed her down a passage.

'Why did you say we missed the bus?' whispered Sandra. 'I thought we went because of the police lady?'

'She wouldn't have understood,' said Paul unhappily. 'Sssh!'

'Are we really going to our Gran's for a holiday, like you said?'

'In a way, yes.'

She looked at him, puzzled, but did not pursue the matter.

In the warm kitchen, with the background noise of talk, clinking glasses, and soft music from the bar, the woman plied them with cake and biscuits, chatting all the time.

'You know it's come back to me now who she reminds me of, your little sister. As soon as I saw her I knew there was someone . . . She's the image of a little girl we had here once. Lynn, she was called. She'd have been just about the same age when she was here. She was an evacuee from London, you see – it was during the war. You know how they sent them away from the cities, to get away from the bombing? Poor little mites – they were so small, some of them, to go off on their own like that, away from everything they knew, dumped down with strangers. Of course, up to five they went with their mothers, but older than that they were on their own. Lynn wasn't much older – I never saw anything so pathetic. We went to Banbury to get them – us from the village that had said we'd have children billeted with us. They had them all in a church hall there, all tired out with travelling, sitting on their bundles with labels round their necks like so many parcels, and you just went round and said, "I'll have that one". Poor souls – I've never forgotten how they looked. Like little lost animals, all staring at you hoping someone would pick them, and brothers and sisters trying to make sure they stayed together, holding on to each other. Lynn was on her own: I think I picked her because she was the wretchedest looking of them all. Like a puppy that had been beaten.'

She sat down at the table, stirring a cup of tea. Sandra was stroking the cat curled up in front of the stove like a black bun. Paul tried to look interested: at least this person wasn't asking questions any more now.

'Have another slice of cake, dear? What was I saying? Oh, poor little Lynn. Yes, we had a dreadful time with her to begin with, though she settled down in the end. She even ran off once, on a night rather like this – all foggy, and we found her a couple of miles away, down the green lane, down the Old Driftway, babbling away to herself as though she were a bit touched in the head, poor child. But it was after that she settled down.'

Mrs Larkins wiped her hands on a towel, took off her apron, and sat down. 'There! It's been one of those days, all go from morning to night. No rest for the wicked, is there? I daresay you could do with your bed, too, dear.'

Paul was staring at her. 'Where did you say you found her?'

'Found who, dear?'

'The girl. Lynn.'

'Oh, along the green lane a mile or so back. It's an old road, you know, but it isn't used now. Yes, it was a dreadful evening, I'll never forget it. She'd been with us three or four days, I suppose, and she was frantic for her mother. She never said anything, nor cried, but you could see she was desperate, if you knew anything about children. I was at my wits' end, I couldn't do anything for her. I tried everything I knew, I was that sorry for her, but it was no good. She didn't want food, nor love, nor anything, she just wanted to go home. We were so upset: I mean, you don't like to have someone being so unhappy when they're in your house, do you? You feel so helpless. Well, anyway, suddenly about six o'clock one evening we realized she'd disappeared. We hunted all over, but we couldn't find her, and I rang up the billeting officer, and the police, and we had all the village out looking for her, all the evening, and I went out hunting for her myself with a hurricane lamp, and I found her huddled in the hedge along the green lane, wet through, and chattering away for the first time since she'd come – she'd hardly said a word till that moment. She went on and on about a man telling her a story. We couldn't make it out at all, because it wasn't anyone from round here – I mean, we know everyone – and the way she described it you really had to think she'd dreamed it or something. A man on a horse with a long cloak – it was ridiculous. Anyway, we took her home and put her to bed and the funny thing was she was all right after that, she settled down and she stayed with us quite happy till nearly the end of the war. But she had a thing about that road ever after that: she was always going off down there on her own, and coming back in quite a paddy – she had a bit of a temper, did Lynn – as though she'd not been able to get something she wanted.'

'What's happened to her now?' said Paul.

'Oh, we kept in touch after the war. She went back to the East End, where she'd come from, Stepney, but she used to come to us for her holidays sometimes. She loved it here. In fact she was down this summer. She's married now, of course, with a couple of children of her own. Funny, you know I've just remembered, the first thing she had to do when they came was go for a walk down that road. She dragged them all off, and her husband was grumbling away at her – he was a real townie, didn't care for walking at all – but she wouldn't take any notice of him. She went marching off down there. It was almost as though she was looking for something.'

Paul pushed his plate to one side. He'd eaten the cake without noticing, he found.

'Finished, dear? Would you like to wash your hands or anything? Wake up, love! – You're not listening to a word I'm saying, are you?'

'Sorry,' said Paul. 'It was just – oh, nothing really. What did you say he was like – the man who told her a story?'

Mrs Larkins was swilling cups under the tap. 'Oh, I forget, dear. But there wasn't anyone really, you see. It was all in her mind. Must have been, mustn't it?'

Paul said nothing. He walked over and looked out of the window: outside cars ploughed through the darkness, passing the pub with a faint sighing noise, as though the fog dulled sound as well as sight.

'Nasty night,' said Mrs Larkins. 'I don't like these autumn fogs. You can feel quite stifled. Well, we'd better see how old Bill's getting on, hadn't we?'

Bill was just putting the finishing touches to the shaft. Mr Larkins came out of the pub door just as they reached the yard.

'Off, are you, Bill? All shipshape now?'

'As good as I can make her,' said Bill. 'Thanks a lot.'

'Don't mention it. Hello there, young lady. My, Annie, she's got quite a look of our Lynn, hasn't she?'

'Just what I was saying to her brother. Now, Bill, you get them to their Gran's as quick as you can, won't you? I'm not all that happy about them. I'd have liked to have them taken on in a car, I really would.' She lowered her voice a

95

little. 'I've got this feeling there's something not quite right. The boy ... He's a nice lad, but there's something on his mind. You can tell that.' They stood staring, the man and the woman, their kindly faces furrowed with concern, waving after the cart as it creaked out of the yard and into the darkness.

'Decent folk,' said Bill. 'Hearts in the right place. Not like some.'

'Where are some people's hearts, then?' said Sandra, squinting down at her chest.

Bill laughed. 'They got left out, I reckon. But I shouldn't worry about yours. You'll do. And this feller-me-lad, when he gets himself sorted out.'

Paul looked sharply at him, but the old man was busy with his pipe, sucking and puffing.

'She told me about someone else who'd – who'd heard things on the road. The messages. But she didn't understand – Mrs Larkins didn't, I mean. She thought the person had just imagined it.'

'Ah,' said Bill. 'Well, it's hard to credit, isn't it? For some.'

They turned out of the yard and into the road once more.

'Will the shaft be all right now?' said Paul.

'She should last out. Tell you what, since you've got such a fancy for the old tracks there's another short cut we can take here where the new road leaves the old 'un.'

Paul said, 'Good.' The more they could stay off the road, the better, even if it took longer. He wanted to get to Gran's, but at the same time he wanted to put it off: he wanted more time to deal with things that were going on in his mind. Uncertainties, confusions, questions that kept uncurling themselves, muddling him.

The clamour of Bessie's feet hitting the tarmac ceased

abruptly, muted to a soft thud as they turned once more into a lane.

'There,' said Bill. 'This'll take us half a mile or so. It's queer to think this was once a road for strangers, travellers. You only get local folk using the green roads now.'

'Green roads,' said Paul. 'I like that.'

'They were all green once. Now there's just a few left like this one – ghost roads, so to speak. I use 'em a lot.'

'Go on,' said Paul.

'Eh?'

'Go on like you did before. About travelling, and seeing the shape of the country, and all that.'

'Ah. You've taken a fancy to that kind of thing, have you? But you know there's something else about my way of travelling, and to my mind it's the most interesting part of all, and that's that you're not just moving through places, you're moving through people. You see how a man in one town's different from a man in another: acts different, thinks different. You hear how there's a hundred different ways of talking English, and you see how people stick to the places they've come from, for the most part. People have roots, like trees. They stay in one place, for hundreds of years. The same village, or the same bit of a city. They couldn't tell you why, and neither could I, but that's the way it is.'

'My Gran's always lived in Cold Higham. And there's old tombstones in the churchyard with the same name on as ours. She showed me once. We went to live in Banbury because my dad got a job there.'

'But he'd not go further, I daresay. Unless he'd not got a choice.'

'I don't think so.'

'This is the middle bit of England here. The Midlands. It's a good word, that. It's got a solid feeling to it, but at the same time you know it's a place related to other places. The north and the south, and Wales, and the east, and the sea. That's why it's such an old part: used since right back, and travelled over, and built on, and fought over, time and again.'

'That boy,' said Paul. 'Cynric.'

'He was only one of many as had to fight just for the right to stay put. Before people started fighting about more complicated things. About ways of thinking, and that. Know anything about the Civil War?'

'Not much. Just about Roundheads and Cavaliers, and that sort of thing.'

'That was going on all around here. Oxford and Banbury, and Reading. There was a battle fought just the other side of Banbury. Edgehill, it was called. A horrible business. Men fighting others that spoke the same language, knew the same things. People whose faces they could recognize. It's hard to think about.'

'It's hard to think of fighting going on round here. Places we've been through today. I mean, it's as though nothing had ever happened, for a thousand years.' Fields, brown and cream and green, the melting shapes of trees, hedges, zigzagging away into the distance, folding into one another, rooks, pigeons, silence. 'What would a battle be like? Really and truly. For someone in it?'

'Not like anything we think,' said Bill. 'Not like cowboys and Indians on the telly. Nor yet like what's written in books, either. That's put together afterwards, with people writing down what they think happened, so that it comes out tidylike. To my mind it wouldn't be like that at the time. It would be a right old mess, and nasty, too.'

'That old lady we had tea with,' said Paul. 'She said her husband lived there all his life except just for the bit when he went to fight in France.'

'That's how it's been for a good many people. Just once in their lives they get pitched into something big like that, through no choice of their own. A person's life gets mixed up with what's happening in the world. And then there's no escaping it.'

Bill fell silent, his chin tucked down into the scarf round his neck, his sharp nose tipped with a rosette of red light reflected from the lantern, the wrinkles on his face etched in with shadows like black scars. Sandra was asleep, slumped in her nest of sacks and coats. Paul watched the hedges slide past on either side: beyond them there was nothing but white mist.

And then all of a sudden something moved under a sapling in the hedge, too slowly for bird or rabbit, too deliberately for a swaying branch. He looked, first with an idle curiosity, and then with an intense concentration: it commanded attention in a way that he was beginning to recognize. If it was another of these messages, then he had to capture it: it must not be allowed to get away.

They were passing it. He grabbed Bill's arm and said urgently, 'Please – could we stop a moment? There's something in the hedge there ... I must see.'

The old man grunted. Then he jerked at the reins and pulled Bessie to a halt. 'Right you are, son, if it means so much to you.'

Paul slid down from the cart. Beyond the circle of light from the lantern there was a clammy blackness where wet grass and overhanging branches made vicious snatches at feet and head, and the ground fell away disconcertingly into ditches and ruts. He advanced into it, stumbling.

The movement came again, and it was a foot. Two feet, booted and muddy, sticking from the hedge. He moved a little closer, stealthily, and then closer still, and beyond the feet there was a body, arms and head, sprawled half in the

99

hedge, flung down as though in utter exhaustion, with no regard for comfort or convenience. It was a young man, fair-haired, with beard and moustache, dressed in dirty leather breeches, tattered shirt, high-cuffed boots, and black armour back and front. A sword and pot-shaped helmet were thrown down beside him. He was fast asleep.

And then, as Paul looked, breathless, the young man flung out an arm, and murmured something, his eyes still closed. Paul strained to hear, and a voice, a little slurred with sleep, but nonetheless a plain, ordinary voice, came to him from the hedge.

It said, 'William? Is that you, brother?'

Paul said, in a whisper, 'Yes.'

7

It's strange I should dream of you now, brother, for in the extremities of this day I have thought it all a dream, as though in truth I were back with you at Colchester and indulging myself with idle fantasy. But no fantasy could be as strange as this day has been, nor as horrible. Do you remember how we played battles when we were boys? How we drew up our men in lines like trees upon a hill, and marched them hither and thither, and fired upon each other, and re-formed and fired again, and counted our losses, and thereby declared victory or defeat ...? All as neat and well-contrived as a game of chess. We knew nothing, William, nothing. A battle's another matter altogether, and one in which all contriving's gone to the winds from the instant of the first advance, lost in noise, smoke, and confusion. And reality itself's a victim of that same confusion: for what's victory to one man may seem defeat to another, even though they fight side by side. They told me up the road just now that my Lord Essex has claimed the day, that we who fought for Parliament have won. Victory. But victory's a matter for exultation, is it not? And I, for my part, never felt so crushed and weakened as a man, seeing what I've seen today and knowing what I now know, that the conception of a matter can be turned to ashes by the fact.

The place where we fought was called Edgehill, by a small town called Kineton, some few miles from here. I'll remember the name all my life, for it's where I've learned that we cannot be always private men, but that to all of us, or to most, there comes a time when what we do, and what we become, is bound up with matters beyond our control, whether we like it or not. And a battle's a very perfect example of that. At one moment I'm Matthew Cobham, son of William Cobham of Colchester, a plain and private man, standing behind a hedge on a fine autumn day, with the sky over my head and grass under my feet, and the next I'm but a mark on a piece of paper, telling of how many fought at the battle of Edgehill, and how many were slain, and how many were in this troop and how many in that. And the day that stands high in my fortunes as a private man, stands high also in the fortunes of my country, and so the two are become one, in a way I had not foreseen, going about my business in Colchester and in London.

You know that I joined Master Denzil Holles' force in June, offering myself as a musketeer, believing as I then did that it was no longer possible for a man of conscience to stand aside in the struggle between King and Parliament. The smell of violence was in the air. I wanted, as did all reasonable men, a peaceable resolution to our troubles: I came to think, as did most, that this was no longer possible, that the King by his actions had eroded our most precious liberties and that there was nothing left but to take up arms against him. And so through the heat of summer I learned my business as a musketeer: learned how to fire, and how to re-load, how to keep my match always burning, to turn from the wind so that the priming powder should not be blown away, to stow a bullet in my mouth for quicker loading in action. I learned the business of firing by intro-duction – how to take my place in the file of six men, fire upon the order as he in front fell back, and fall back in turn myself. And I learned too what an ill-matched bunch were my companions – drawn to the fight for every reason you can conceive of, from the hope of gain to the burning of religious faith. And it came to me that this is a war of opinion, but it is fought by a people accustomed to wars of loyalty, and that this perhaps accounts for the terrible perplexity in which we find ourselves, for they say the whole country is a patchwork of loyalties and beliefs.

In July we left London and marched towards Worcester to join the main body of my Lord Essex' force. 'March' is too fine a word, though, for that long, wet, slow, cumbersome drag through the tracks and lanes of midland England, sweating under the sun one moment, shivering in the rain the next, halting to heave artillery and equipment through the mud, plaguing private citizens for food and drink, stealing, destroying ... At Worcester we waited as summer lengthened into autumn, and those of us who were countryfolk thought of harvest, and the more profitable occupations of private men. All around us the corn ripened, and fell before the sickle, apples flushed the trees, leaves turned yellow and dropped, and ordinary people went about their ordinary business: only the gentry scurried here and there with troubled faces, for it was become scarcely possible for any man of standing to remain uncommitted, for his own safety's sake, and that of his estates. And then at last there came the news that the King's army was but twenty miles away, moving south from Warwick.

The order to march reached our company, quartered in a village just beyond the outskirts of the town, as the main body of the army was already gathered up and moving, like some sluggish insect that shifts one part of itself and then another. The cottage folk in whose homes and barns we'd camped ourselves were not sad to see us go: they'd been reluctant hosts, with no choice in the matter. I remember a child who stared as we clattered into a rainy dawn, tramping through mud past cows and chickens, reminders of a more tranquil world: I can see its wide eyes now, and the apple in its hand. Pray God it lives to grow up in better times.

We marched four days: a worse progress than the first, over roads churned into mire by the autumn rains and the progress of our own front part. We laboured over carts axle-deep in mud, and horses sunk to their quarters, bawled at by sergeants, wet to the bone and cursing like the old troopers we'd become. At night we quartered ourselves as best we could, sometimes with no better than a hedge for cover, and nothing in our bellies but biscuits and a knob of cheese. Those among us without scruples took what they could from farm and cottage: eggs, milk, meat. I saw a poor woman stand watching, silent, children huddled to her skirts, as half a dozen fellows stripped her farmhouse bare and rode away into the night.

On the fourth evening, late, at the end of a weary day, we trudged into Kineton to find ourselves caught up with the rest, and the whole place alive with men searching for food, shelter, fodder for horses, blacksmiths and information. For news was what we clutched at most greedily, and what was hardest to come by: news of where we should go next, and when, of where the enemy lay, and how strong he was. For my own part, weary and hungry as I was, I was still consumed with eagerness to come to grips with the war: it seemed to shuffle on the edge of my existence, like some threatening spectre, to be disposed of only by confrontation. And so I wandered in the darkness, among the sullen spitting fires lit by the wayside, and past the cottage windows glowing orange from a candle within, seeking to acquaint myself with what was known. The people in those parts were for Parliament, though for no other reason but that they are tenants of Lord Saye and align their loyalties with his: they watched us with wary eyes, having been much milked already, and too familiar with the soldier who takes food and promises payment later. Rumours abounded: that the King was already on the road for London, that he had retreated north, that he was twenty miles away, or three, or fifty. But the strongest opinion had it that Lord Essex was resolved to march next day to the relief of the garrison at Banbury, and so, with orders to parade before dawn next morning, we set ourselves down for the night, to seize what rest we could.

The drums aroused us in darkness. I stumbled from the barn where I'd lain with my companions and some steaming cows, buckled on my armour and took up my musket. We assembled in a lane beyond the church, and stood in the cold dawn to await the inspection of a surly sergeant: I watched light streak the sky beyond the rooftops, stamped my cold feet to move the blood, and remembered happier dawns, brother, when you and I rose early for a day's hawking on the moors beyond our home. The whole town whispered with the movement of men, for the main body of the army was quartered there, and thereabouts, though it was said our numbers were short by three regiments of foot, and several troops of horse, who'd not yet reached the place. We saw our commanders ride by to attend a service at the church, and then there was much coming and going of officers in haste, riding to and fro while the sky brightened all the while and the night gave way to day, and we stamped and grumbled and regretted our empty stomachs. And then came the word – how, I hardly know, except that it spread like fire crackling through a field of stubble – that the King's army was drawn up but a mile from the town, at a place called Edgehill. And no sooner had we learned this than the command came to march from where we were and draw up in order of battle in the open field which lay to the south of the town, at the foot of this hill.

There was no confusion. The army streamed from the

narrow lanes that left the town, and dispersed upon the fields beyond, for the place was flat and open, save for some briars and enclosures to the right. And indeed, in the exhilaration of the moment, an army seemed to me a brave sight, with the sun glittering on a thousand pikes, the standards rolling in the wind, and all the sounds of drum, trumpet, and the thud of horses' hooves. It was a fine, clear day, and we could see the sharp rise of the hill to the south, whereon the King's force had taken up its position, and it was clear to me that it was too steep for us to make an attack, but that we must wait for the enemy to descend, and indeed that was our commanders' intent also, for we began to draw up at the base of the hill, unhindered by the enemy, whose movements we could clearly see, coming and going upon the summit.

Some four hundred men of Mr Holles' foot, of whom I was one, were placed to the left of the main body of our horse, well in advance of the front line, to flank our force and give fire to theirs, to the 'Forlorn Hope' as they call the first rank of the advance. We were ranged behind a hedge, with some ordnance concealed in our midst, and between us and the enemy lay nothing but a reach of open ground, striped green and buff with grass and cut corn. I think that when we saw this our spirits sank a little: there's not many relish the thought of being flung first into a fight, but our leaders, not unaware of this, devoted much time to our company, riding to and fro all that morning exhorting us, encouraging, and declaiming against the enemy as Papists, Atheists, and Irreligious Persons. The hours crawled by: we could see the enemy dispose himself on the hillside before us, though not near enough to determine which regiment stood where, or how their horse were placed, but from time to time we saw a standard raised, and once even were able to observe the progress of the King and his advisers, by the cheers and shouts that came from those near him as he passed. All this long wait took its toll amongst us: men whose determination was in doubt became more and more uneasy, spreading their discontent to others like a pox. There was a lad of my file, Tom Summers by name, only sixteen years of age, who'd enlisted by way of a jape, to prove himself before his friends: I remember him vomiting on the grass, white-faced. For my part, I leaned up against the hedge, and allowed myself to become very close acquainted with a swag of briar, counting the mildewed berries, observing the shape and structure of the leaves, taking note of the behaviour of a spider who had her house slung between two twigs. In that way I kept my fear pushed under.

Towards midday the enemy advanced down the hill, and drew up at the foot, and not long after our ordnance opened fire. For an hour or more the guns answered one another, without much damage being done either side, serving only to obscure the day with smoke. My own fear swelled up, as the clear view I had before me vanished into fog, out of which could come one knew not what: if I was to die, I wanted at least the opportunity to fire a shot before. And then the guns were silent. I saw the sergeant staring over the hedge into the smoke, eyes screwed up, heard him give the order to load, which I did as though in a dream, and then we waited.

We heard them before we saw them, the rattle of the harness and the hoof-beats – a troop of dragoons coming upon us from the front. I dropped to my knees and fired upon the order, and then fell back. There was time for two more rounds of fire, and then they were upon us: I saw a section of the hedge go down before two horses, and poor Tom Summers with it, slashed by a sword, rolling away into a muddy ditch. I never set eyes on him again. I was re-loaded now, but they were all among us, with swords and pistols out, and more coming up behind: I heard them bawling, and it was like a sudden blow to hear an Essex voice, and then a London one. The noise was fearful, of pistol shots, and blows, and the sound of men screaming. I tried to fire again, but found all targets too dispersed, and then there was a fellow riding at me with his sword up-raised, but even as my stomach turned to water I knew to swing my musket round and have at him with the butt end, so that the blow fell on his sword arm and he wheeled away in search of other prey. I saw my companions fall, some shot, some ridden down: I saw another troop of horse advance towards the hedge: and then I knew discretion to be the better part of valour, and began to flee with the rest of our company, back towards our own lines.

They had their way with us in the retreat, picking off men as they wished. All around me others were swearing and panting as they ran, and cursing our own horse for not coming to our defence, but it seemed to me even then that the failure was one of ignorance rather than resolve, for in the black smoke from our own ordnance that now fired again, it was impossible to know what went on more than fifty paces away. Indeed, as we fell back into our own foot, they sent a round of fire among us, thinking us part of the enemy advance until they heard our shouts. I threw myself down into a ditch, to escape our pursuers (though they were now begun to fall back, with their numbers not reinforced, so that it seemed they must be but an advance attack to dispose of our defence), and also to recover myself, for all the breath was gone from me and I could hardly stand. In this position, lying in the mud, I saw to my disgust a lieutenant in Sir Faithfull Fortescue's troop ride forward to the enemy, throwing down his Parliamentary colours and declaring that his commander was resolved to join the other side. I'd lost all the other fellows of my file, and indeed most of those of the company, so interspersed were we now with the main body of our foot (and indeed many, I know, declared at the moment they'd had enough, and were not seen again that day). And even as I clambered from my ditch, and looked around to see how I should position myself once more, I saw our front rank open fire, and saw that the main body of the enemy horse was advancing at the trot.

I've little memory of that charge. I think my mind was numbed from what I'd already seen: I don't remember fear, but I remember thinking with certainty that I should die. I saw others die, on both sides: some disposed of quick by pistol or sword, others, less fortunate, left wounded on the field. I saw our own horse come from the right to meet the charge: I saw the ranks of our foot utterly dispersed, so that men ran hither and thither, deprived of the protection of one another and seeking only their own safety, like a nest of ants stirred up by an intruding straw: I saw a hundred individual battles fought, a hundred victories and defeats – suffered such encounters myself, now with the enemy, now with our own horse, pushed back by theirs and riding blind upon us: I saw courage and panic, treachery and resolve, fear, amazement, bewilderment and confusion: but never for one instant did I see that order, that precision, or that clear purpose which I had understood was the essence of a battle. Indeed, only by the fact that, turning to find out my position, I saw the rooftops of Kineton nearer than they had been before, did I understand that we had lost much ground: and indeed all around now there were our own men falling back, and troops of their horse riding through and beyond, so that it seemed clear to me that the battle was lost, as a result of what I'd seen with my own eyes, and what might have happened a mile away, or what might yet happen, was no more my concern than if it were in another country.

I found myself standing by a copse, I remember. There was a poor fellow on the ground nearby, breathing his last, and a horse, wild with fear, that bolted past without a rider: I looked up into the trees, I saw the blaze of autumn leaves as I'd seen them as a child, engraved upon the sky, and it came to me with all the urgency of truth that I was Matthew Cobham and that I had no place here. The battlefield seemed some hideous product of the imagination, the horrid invention of a depraved mind, and all the energy that I'd brought to bear in making myself part of this public endeavour, I applied now to withdrawing myself once again into the world of a private man: I threw my musket to the ground and ran.

All the rest of the day until darkness fell I stumbled away from the place, hardly knowing where I was but moving all the time in the direction of London: from time to time I saw others with the same purpose, but I kept myself apart from them. I am not yet come to terms with today's events, and cannot talk of it, except to you, brother, in the brief release of a dream: I know only that what I have seen, and what I have learned, must scar me like a branded horse, or even, more than that, leave its mark upon my very nature, making me a different man from that I was before.

The voice ceased abruptly, interrupted by Bill saying something. Paul turned for a moment to look over his shoulder, and when he looked back at the hedge there was no one there, just brown leaves with the mist smoking up through them.

'You coming, son? I said we'd best not hang around too long.'

Paul got back into the cart. 'Was I long?'

'No,' said Bill, 'hardly a moment. Got what you wanted, did you?'

'Yes. Yes, I did.'

'The old road talking again, was it?'

'Yes. There was somebody who fought at that battle. Edgehill. He was a Parliament person. The ones that won. Or at least he said they thought they'd won, but he didn't feel he'd won anything.'

'Why not, then?' Bill nudged Bessie into movement. Paul glanced back for a moment. The place where Matthew Cobham had been had already vanished into darkness. But he was not there anyway: he was a mark on a piece of paper, wasn't he? A list of names and numbers, to do with a battle, a long time ago.

'Well, I suppose just because it wasn't what he'd expected it would be. It made him feel awful, not glorious or anything.'

'What was he doing, then?'

'Going away,' said Paul. 'He just wanted to get away. Not think about it.'

'Ah. Stands to reason. But he'd have to in the end.'

'Have to what?'

'Think about it. Deal with it in his head. When a thing's happened to you it's no good shoving it away and pretending it hasn't. You can go off your nut that way.'

'Battles?'

'Not just battles,' said Bill with a snort. 'Most of us don't get mixed up with battles, do we? Anything. Everything.'

Everything?

'It's what you do about things that makes you the kind of bloke you are,' said Bill. 'Eh? The way you deal with 'em or not. Get up, Bessie! By, it's a right thick fog, this.'

What you do about things. Or don't do. Paul stared into the night: ahead, lights swam across the darkness – a motorbike, tearing the silence, a bus, cruising the night, its brightness furred by the mist.

'There,' said Bill, 'we've met up with the road again.'

They turned out of the lane and on to hard tarmac. Sandra woke up and stared round.

'What's that shining thing?'

'Just a bus.'

'Oh. Is it the bus Gran comes to see us on?'

'Could be.' The question brought Paul back to things that had been tugging away in his head all day. Gran. Dad. Her. No, Christine. She's got a name, hasn't she? She's a person, isn't she? Gran ... It was a good thing she didn't know anything about all this, because she'd have got fussed. Old people worry about things. She'd get a shock when they turned up, out of the blue like that. He'd have to try to make it less of a shock, somehow. Maybe he'd better go into Mrs Lang next door first, not just walk in at Gran's straight away.

And I'll have to get a message to Dad and Christine: they'll have been dead worried.

I've been daft, he thought, I really have. There, I've said it. Only to myself, but I've said it. Instead of just gabbling on about something else so as not to think about it too much. Daft about not telling them where we were going, and daft about going at all, I think.

And daft about other things, too, maybe.

They rounded a bend, and suddenly there was confusion ahead. A lorry was slewed across the road: red lights, haloed in mist, winked from the rear of a line of waiting cars: a policeman, incandescent in white overalls, stood in the middle of the road directing the traffic: a police car was parked on the verge, its radio chattering from the empty interior.

Paul clutched the rim of the cart: his stomach melted: the lights ahead seemed to spin.

'Accident,' said Bill. 'You get them, these foggy nights. Hope there's no one hurt. I can't see no ambulance.'

They joined the queue of cars moving slowly by the lorry, twisted back on itself like a fractured limb, and a small car pushed into the hedge with the bonnet dented. Paul watched the police car, mesmerized by the murmur of the radio. What was it saying?

'Why,' said Bill suddenly, dragging on the reins, 'if it isn't my old mate, Tom Hopkins. Whoa up there, Bessie! Evening, Tom! How're you keeping?'

Another policeman, standing beside a motorbike writing something down on a pad, turned round. 'Hello there, Bill! Thought it must be your circus I saw. There's no one else on the road with an outfit quite like yours, eh?' His glance roved across the children.

'What's up?' said Bill, waving his whip in the direction of the lorry. 'Bad?'

'No one hurt,' said the policeman. 'Damage to vehicles only. You'll always get the odd lunatic going faster than he ought in the fog. Tell me, Bill, you get around these parts, do you know anything about ...' His voice trailed away as he leaned towards Bill and the two of them talked quietly. Bill had pulled the cart into the wide of the road: the slow-moving line of cars crawled past them.

Paul's eyes were fixed on the police car. A policeman had got into it and was talking into a microphone: it was not possible to hear what he said.

Two men were standing by the lorry, hands thrust in their pockets, watching the traffic: one of them, in oil-stained overalls, appeared to be the driver. Fragments of their conversation reached Paul.

'... can't move without a new rear axle. And they take

their time at our depot in Northampton ... should be here any minute now.'

'How did it happen?'

'Couple of blokes in that Mini ... belting round the corner like a bat out of hell ... put my foot down but I could see they were heading for the ditch.'

'What happened to them?'

'Made off. It was a stolen car, see. The law knew all about them – couple of blokes on the run – they'd had half a dozen cars since this morning. There'd been something on the radio ...'

'Why are we waiting here?' said Sandra. 'I want to go.'

'Sssh.' He was only half-listening to the men talking. It was the policeman in the car that interested him. He had a nice face: well, just kind of ordinary-looking. A face that might sell you sweets in a sweet-shop, or belong to the person next door, or smile at you in a bus: it looked the kind of face that, if you went and explained things to it, would open up and look understanding and interested, not clam up and shut you off. If you took off his hat, and didn't look at his uniform, he mightn't have been a policeman at all. Suppose, just suppose he got down and went over there and asked him the time or something, and then if he still seemed nice, just suppose he told him what had happened, right from the very beginning ... About how it had all been a mistake, and he hadn't meant to take those things in the shop, and he'd got in a panic with the policewoman, and been stupid and run off ... Suppose he did that, was there any chance it might be all right? That they might just forget about the whole thing? Not tell Dad and Christine, not put him in prison or anything? He'd never been all that sure they did that, anyway, just for pinching things in a shop. Trouble is, he thought, I kind of built it all up in my mind, didn't I? I do that sometimes. Make things seem quite different from the way they really are.

He watched the policeman intently, chewing his lip. Bill and the other one were still talking, standing a few yards away beside the hedge. Paul swung his legs over the edge of the cart and slid to the ground.

'Where are you going?' said Sandra. 'Can't I come?'

'Ssh. I won't be a minute. Just wait.'

8

He edged his way between two cars. There was a break-down truck lifting the Mini from the ditch, and the police-man was sitting watching it, drumming his fingers on the driving-wheel. Paul went slowly towards him, uncertain, half-wishing he'd never started, and then suddenly another policeman appeared from nowhere, got into the passenger seat, and said something inaudible.

The first one said, 'We'll get back then.' He started the engine, and began to reverse on to the road.

Paul opened his mouth, and hesitated. The police-man saw him, rolled down the window, and said sharply, 'Get back in your car, son. It's not safe wandering around the road in this fog.' He revved the engine, and drove off.

Paul felt a moment of disappointment, which quickly became relief. It had been a stupid idea: he'd been jolly lucky, really. Fancy thinking they'd have listened to him: they'd have done no such thing, not on your life, they wouldn't. They'd have whipped him straight off to wher-ever they whipped you off to, and that would have been that. There'd have been no chance to explain to Dad, or anyone, that was for sure. No, it had been jolly lucky they'd gone off before he had a chance to say anything, jolly lucky. The best thing was to go on just as they were, if he could manage it. He looked round for Bill.

The old man was just climbing on to the cart again. 'Well, cheero then, Tom. I'd better be on my way. I've got passengers tonight.'

The policeman swung himself on to the saddle of the motorbike. 'Cheero, Bill. Be seeing you, eh?' He glanced at Paul, who had been trying to reach the cart unnoticed, but did not speak to him. He started the motorbike and rode away, talking into the radio as he went. Bill lifted the reins.

'Get up, then, Bess!'

They moved away down the road, away from the island of light and activity round the lorry and into the darkness beyond. Paul turned once to look back: no one followed them except cars which quickly passed and were swallowed up once more. They were alone again, to all intents and purposes. He was filled with relief: that had been a near escape, it really had. He'd been stupid. He was tired, that was the trouble, and being tired was making him get silly ideas. No, he'd been right in the first place, clearing out when he had, not being taken in by that policewoman pretending to be all friendly. He gritted his teeth and stared aggressively into the darkness.

'Nice bloke, Tom Hopkins,' said Bill. 'Been around here for five years or so now. We often have a chat. He did me a good turn once when some young wretches turned my donkeys loose and chased 'em all over the country. Went to a lot of trouble to get 'em back for me, Tom did.'

Paul muttered something.

'Eh?'

'I said, he's still a policeman, isn't he?'

'By, you do like to slap labels on people, don't you?'

Paul hunched his shoulders under his anorak and moved away slightly: it's not fair, everybody turns against you just when you think they're on your side. Like Gran. It's just not fair.

'No offence meant,' said Bill. 'And none taken, I hope. Eh?'

Paul said nothing. He felt tired now, really tired. He

117

wished he could go to sleep, like Sandra, but he was too fussed for that: he felt again like he'd felt at the start of this journey, stiff and anxious, with noises too loud and lights too bright: he had to blink and turn his head away every time a car swept by. The road was busier again, and from time to time they passed a cottage or farm. Now they were following the long curve of a high stone wall. He could see his own shadow flapping against it, travelling with them, and now suddenly coming towards him as it was thrown back by the headlights of a car: he stared, fascinated, as it seemed to harden and take shape, advancing towards him, revealing the outline of his hands, his face in profile, the jutting hood of his anorak . . .

. . . And a cloak trailing behind, and the butt of a pistol, tucked into a belt, and a three-cornered hat, and high boots. And now it had frozen against the wall, and become more real than the wall itself, or the road, or the cart, so that everything else seemed to hang round it, as though he and it were suspended alone in the night, imprisoned together in the momentary flood of light from a car not yet visible beyond the corner. And in that instant he felt impelled to confront it, to stop it, to make demands of it, so that he leaned forward and (he thought) spoke to it (but, he knew later, could only have spoken in his mind, for Bill did not turn his head, nor did Sandra stir).

He said, 'Did you kill the third drover? Or did the other two?'

You've perceived then that there's more than one side to the coin (the shadow said), that the tale may not be such as it appears at the first telling, for the truth of an affair has many facets, like a diamond, and shines different according to whose eyes are cast upon it. There's no doubt but that evil was done, but what was the nature of the crime, and against whom was it committed? Hear my story, and decide for yourself.

They call me Driftway Jim, but I was born James Tobias Hooker, of the parish of Woodstock, in Oxfordshire. I'll not trouble you with the history of my progress towards my present condition, save to say that it became apparent to me at an early age that this life's but a game of devil-take-the-hindmost, and that he's best served who serves himself. Moreover, discovering in myself a natural distaste both for poverty and for hard work, I determined that it would best become me to discard those scruples induced in me by a gentle upbringing and set about the furtherance of my interests in any way that seemed profitable. Being the son of a gentleman, though not, unfortunately, a man of means, those opportunities open to me were connected for the most part with gaming, betting and the like. I tried my hand as a cardsharper, and at the various doubtful practices connected with the sport of horse-racing, but found myself more often than not outwitted by others whose skill in these matters was greater than my own.

And so, after several years, I have come to my present pursuit, a profession which is well known to induce a short life, but which has afforded me much satisfaction, enabling me as it does to effect a more equal redistribution of that wealth which I have always felt to be improperly concen-trated in the hands of persons other than myself. I relieve ladies of their pearls, and gentlemen of their purses: in this way I lighten their material burdens and bring them closer to spiritual salvation, while at the same time making avail-able to myself that style of life to which I feel I am naturally entitled. Furthermore, my exploits are a source of interest and of pleasure to the humble people of the countryside, who see me as in some way a challenge to that ordering of society which condemns them always to have the least and suffer the most without being in any way able to influence their condition. For I am careful only to rob the rich: not, let me hasten to inform you, because of any delicacy of feeling about the evils of poverty, but because I am well aware that it is the silence and the sympathy of the ordinary people that protects me from the officers of the law who will, sooner or later, string me up by the neck on the gallows at Tyburn.

But allow me to return to this matter of the Welsh drover, my friend, that you may judge for yourself how the truth is distorted. Now my first acquaintance with the affair was when a lad they call Tom, who's in my pay, came to me one night at an inn beyond Culworth where I'm accustomed to dine, and told me there was a Welshman would speak to me on a matter of the utmost importance. I should add that Tom's a cunning rascal who feigns idiocy the better to spy for me along the road, and keep me informed of who travels, when, and where: he brings me good custom and costs me little, for he's a pauper boy and kept happy with a coin or two. I left my dinner to grow cold, and went to speak to this fellow in the yard. A hulking brute he was, black and shaggy as an ox, and speaking an English so mauled-about I was hard put to it at first to understand his business: but when finally I was able to penetrate the thickets of his speech, what I heard greatly aroused my interest, so that I ordered ale to be brought for the creature, and urged him to continue with his story.

He was in partnership, it appeared, with a fellow-countryman and an English cattle-dealer named Big Sam, but it had come about that he and the other Welshman had quarrelled, and now this fellow and Big Sam were thick as thieves in alliance against him, to such a degree that he feared not only for his profits when they should have disposed of their drove, but even for his life. All this he recounted to me, brandishing his hairy hands in my face to demonstrate his anxiety, for your Welshman is nothing if not a storyteller, and then at last he came to the nub of the affair. Being a crafty rogue, he proposed to turn the tables on his enemies in this manner: the murder (if murder there was to be) must perforce be planned to take place on the journey back to Wales. At a certain point on the journey, near to where we now stood, he had it in mind to give his friends the slip, leaving them to think what they might: when this was done, he would give me word, and then, he suggested, slanting his black eyes towards me from under those jutting brows, I should fall upon them on the road, remove the booty (one-third of which was his by rights) and share it out between us. If I felt so inclined, he added, I might dispose of his companions into the bargain – it was all one to him.

Observing him to be a person singularly untroubled by problems of morality, I demanded why, in that case, he did not do the job himself? He spread his hands and cringed: there were two of them, look you, and he did not consider he could act swift enough to attend to both at once. Moreover – with a glance at my pistols – he was not properly armed for such an endeavour, and doubted he might come off the worse.

I reflected. What had I to lose by falling in with his proposal? Granted, it might be a trick. It might be that all three were in league together: on the other hand, it seemed to me that the rascal's agitation was not feigned. Furthermore, I had sufficient confidence in my own greater experience in these matters to expect that I might easily enough outwit even three of them. I've robbed drovers before, and know them for a cowardly breed: what is more, this country is my terrain – I know it like I know the lines upon my face, and can turn the knowledge to my advantage.

Accordingly, we struck a bargain: Black Gwyn (for that was his name) would continue his journey, acting all sweet and unsuspecting with his partners, they would do their business at Smithfield, and on such a day (or thereabouts) I would hold myself ready to meet with him again at a certain spot, when he would have abandoned the other two. I feared that his departure might inflame their suspicions, but he assured me no: they would think merely that he was grown wise to their intentions and had sought to save his skin while yet he might.

As chance would have it, I saw the drove pass by the next day, while I lurked in a copse that adjoins the Driftway: three or four hundred head of cattle, running all dispersed across the width of the track so that one fancied a whole black river to flow before the eyes. I observed them with satisfaction, their condition and number being now of some personal interest to me, and was glad to see them excellent fat and healthy: I watched their drovers, too, riding fore and aft, and bade them a silent farewell till we should meet again.

Black Gwyn came to me at the appointed place, and upon the very day he'd promised, breaking out of the dusk like a thunderstorm come up in a fine summer's sky. I was not displeased to see him. Business had been bad of late: I was low in funds and of a mind to remove my pitch from these parts, for I had it on good authority that a certain Sir Thomas Templer, of Throckton Manor, was resolved to bring about my arrest, being desirous to rid the countryside of such a threat to honest folk. Pah! I cared not a jot for Sir Thomas Templer, but rumour had reached me too that he'd brought in a body of peace officers especially for the hunt, armed and horsed, and offering a high price on my head, which latter would be bound in time to tempt the silence of my friends up and down the local inns. I'd resolved, therefore, to make this one last snatch, and then remove myself to some other part of the country, and there lie low to enjoy the proceeds. And so I welcomed my Welsh friend, who told me that his companions lay that night at Culworth, from whence they would proceed early the next morning, and that they had about them nigh on twelve hundred pounds in gold and silver.

I scarce need to tell you that mistrust bloomed between us like flowers in spring: I suspected trickery, Black Gwyn was loath to let me from his sight, knowing full well (I suppose) that I might consider myself entitled to all the plunder once the job was done. Accordingly, we rode together, malevolent companions, following the ways I frequent which enabled me to keep close to the road whilst yet out of sight, our plan being to waylay the victims in a wood beyond Culworth, through which they were bound to pass. It was night as we made the journey, though the moon was high and full to light our path. Once we saw a figure slink like some apparition down the track, and halted in the lee of a great oak until it was gone, thinking of gamekeepers and other persons best avoided at this time, but when the moon shone on his face I saw it to be young Tom, bound no doubt to seek me out and tell me of some likely prey. I let him continue on his fruitless errand, considering it but a just reward for one who chose to keep such bad company.

We were but a mile from our destination when we spied another traveller upon the road, and withdrew again to let him go by: his horse, with the scent of our own in her nostrils, set up a fine to-do so that he was hard pressed to get her past, the which would enable us to observe him close. And what I saw threw me into a fury, and almost had me out upon the road except that Black Gwyn clutched at my arm to hold me back: for what I saw was a mirror of myself, my cloak, my hat, my fine linen, pistol, bandage for the face. Who dared encroach thus upon my pitch! What rogue was this! But Black Gwyn was gabbling in my ear that he knew the fellow, and conjectured that he was about the same business as ourselves: a stable-lad from the inn at Culworth, it seemed, named Jack Trip or some such title, an idle ruffian (he said) who could give us no trouble and, indeed, why not let him do the work for us, and dispose of him when it were done?

I allowed my anger to subside, and thought it would do no harm to follow his suggestion. We let this fellow Trip pass before us, and followed him some way behind, keeping always out of sight. At the point where the road swelled into a clearing in the wood, he withdrew behind some trees, and so did we, and thus did we all three wait as the night lightened into dawn, and then, at last, we heard the hoof-beats of our friends upon the road.

We watched my impersonator fall upon them as to the manner born, and send them scurrying down the track: they gave in with scarce a whimper, as did he to me when I came upon him some minutes later, and drew my pistol as the impertinent wretch slavered over his plunder. My Welsh friend, who'd stood back till now, urged me to blow his brains out, and for an instant I had a mind to do so, until some charitable instinct in me that's not yet quite burned out, prompted me to boot him to his feet and send him yelping down the road instead.

As soon as he was gone I turned my attention to the business in hand: I'd been of a mind, should the opportunity present itself, to seize the Welshman's share and send him packing too, but he'd moved too quick for me and had his hairy fist round the bag of sovereigns before I could do the like, and, what's more, the crafty fellow had the pistol I'd kicked from Jack Trip's grasp, and was scowling at me down the barrel even as I put my hand to my own.

I've been ever of the opinion that the secret of a successful career is the speedy recognition of an unpromising situation: I therefore doffed my hat to him, seized the other bag of coins, and spurred my horse into the woods before he should decide further to exploit his change of fortunes.

A strange night's work, this has been, and a very perfect example of the nature of truth itself, for one person's account of what has happened would be very different from that of another, while each might be true according to the facts as perceived by himself. For my part, I'm well satisfied with the affair: my purse is well-lined, and I cannot help but chuckle as I ride now past the very walls of Sir Thomas Templer's place, to think how I'll cheat him of his hunt for me, for I'll take the road north before ever he hears of this last exploit . . .

Light swept across the wall, pushing the shadow with it, and it became once again the outline of Paul himself, as the car rounded the corner with fog streaming away in front of its headlights. And then it vanished as the car passed and they were alone on the road again.

But now there was something else: a thudding noise that got louder all the time. Paul said, 'There's a horse coming.' He turned to stare back down the road.

'Eh?' said Bill. He might have been dozing, for he sat up suddenly, and tapped Bessie with the whip. 'Steady there, stupid, steady!' The mare was clattering and throwing her head back, so that the cart swayed from side to side: the donkeys, too, were agitated, dragging at their ropes and skittering into the road.

The drumming became louder and louder, it was all round, and so close that it seemed to engulf them: and yet nothing came out of the darkness, and Bill seemed not to hear it but was occupied with Bessie, tugging at the reins and swearing, and Sandra was slumped drowsily against his elbow, eyes half-closed. Noise battered the night, the hoofbeats and the rasping snort of a weary horse, and now suddenly there were other sounds, coming from the right, where the long stone wall ended at a gateway: shouts, footsteps, more horses, the rattle of bridles and stirrups. And now the first hoofbeats had become irregular, confused, halting, and now they were fainter, but the new sounds followed them, passing the cart – so near that Paul found himself crouching down and throwing up his arms to protect himself – passing and surrounding them, horses, creaking leathers, chinking metal, men breathing, calling to one another. And now the noises came from just beyond, and there was the crack of a pistol shot, and another, and another, and the scream of a frightened horse, and the hoofbeats were all dispersed and confused now, but stopped, not going away any more, all milling about on the road . . .

And they ceased: snapped off short. The road was empty: stretching black and wet ahead of them. Bessie shook her head from side to side and settled again into a trot as regular as a pendulum.

'I don't know what comes over her,' said Bill. 'She don't like this stretch of road: I've had her behave like a stupid colt here before.'

Paul stared at him. 'Didn't you hear anything then? Honestly?'

'No, son. I can't say I did. The road been talking to you again, has it?'

'Yes, yes I think so.' The noises were unimaginable now: an instant ago they had been all round, now he could hardly think what they had been like. 'Only in a different way this time. First there was this man telling me about something that happened, and then I think I actually heard what happened next, while it was going on. D'you think that's what upset Bessie?'

'Couldn't rightly say. I wouldn't have thought the old girl upset herself about much except where the next feed's coming from. But there's no knowing, is there? If something strong happened here, maybe she can pick it up too.'

'Where are we?' said Paul.

Bill pointed with his whip towards the wrought-iron gateway they were passing. There were twin stone pillars, topped with stone balls, and lettering incised into the stonework, one word on each pillar. Put together they read Throckton Manor.

'I thought so,' said Paul slowly. 'Yes, that's what I thought.'

'Come to think of it,' said Bill, 'there's one of them stone memorial things on the wall just a bit farther on. I never took the trouble to look at it close. Where is it now? Ah, there it is, under that tree there.'

Paul slid down from the cart. 'Can I see what it says?'

'You'd best take my torch.'

He shone the torch on to the slab of stone let into the high wall. There was moss on it here and there, and a crack across the centre, but it wasn't hard to read.

It said:

On this Spot was Apprehended the Notorious
Highwayman known as DRIFTWAY JIM, otherwise
JAS. TOBIAS HOOKER, who had for many years
Harassed Travellers upon this Road, & who
was Brought to Justice through the Efforts
of a Pauper TOM WINTER of the Parish of
Culworth, who did Inform upon Him. This

Stone was Erected by SIR THO. TEMPLER
to Commemorate the Triumph of Justice
over Villainy & to Record the Diligence
of an Orphan Boy.

14th June, 1743

9

'What's the matter?' said Bill, 'cat got your tongue?' They had gone another mile or so.

'Nothing, really. I was just thinking. The story I told you about earlier – the drovers and the boy from the pub at Culworth, and the highwayman. All that. I know more about it now. You were right: it was different for each person in it, even if what happened was much the same each time. Nobody was quite what the other people thought.'

'Stands to reason,' said Bill. 'Nobody is. That's what makes things interesting. Other people, that is.'

'I'm not sure. You get all muddled. Finding out. You don't know where you are.'

'Ah. But it's if you don't find out you've got something to worry about, son, you take my word for it. Soon as you're ready to believe another bloke might not be exactly what you think he is, you're halfway to being able to live with him. Or work with him, or whatever it is.'

'Or her,' said Paul.

'Or her,' said Bill reflectively. 'Now you take my wife. Twenty-five years we were married, and you'd think in that time you'd have a person pretty well summed-up, wouldn't you? Know what to expect, like. But she could always pull a surprise on me: turn nasty when I thought I'd got her all sweetened up, or take something quite calm-like when I thought we'd have the roof blown off. I liked that: I thought it did her credit.'

Paul thought: take something quite ordinary, because things haven't been for me like they've been for these other people – not murders, and battles, just home, and school. Take coming home from school. Dad's not back yet: Sandra's there first usually, chatting on about what she's been doing, and showing Christine bits of drawing and stuff, and saying 'What's for tea?' And Christine's getting tea – scones and nice things like that – and I come in and maybe something's happened at school I'd like to talk about but when I see her I get all stiff and angry again because that's the way I've always felt about her and when she says 'Did you have a good day, Paul?' I just clam up and go up to my room and that's that.

What's that like for her? Like shouting down a tunnel, probably, with nobody at the other end.

She must feel pretty fed up sometimes. Which makes two of us.

The money in his pocket chinked as the cart lurched, and straightened. I'm glad I didn't get the jug, he thought. Or that stupid padlock.

The fog swept at them in a white wave, and then retreated suddenly, confusingly. A tree that had seemed to stand at the edge of nothingness revealed a background of a wall and a cottage, just visible in the night. The tree itself, flat and rigid like a cardboard cutout, stirred gently as they passed and became a thing of leaves, and branches, and air in between, live and whispering. The fog disguised and distorted. Remove it, and you found everything quite different: you thought yourself in one place and saw it was another. It was as confusing, as abruptly shocking to the senses, as believing one thing to be happening and finding that it might be quite otherwise.

'Are we nearly at Gran's?' said Sandra, sitting up with a jerk.

'Not far off,' said Bill. 'We're getting on. Had enough, have you?'

'It's just I want to be excused.'

'Eh? Oh, I see. By, she likes to talk posh, doesn't she, your little 'un? You'd best take her behind the hedge there. We'll pull into the side a moment. Old Bessie'd like a rest, anyway.'

They scrambled over a ditch and through a hedge, Sandra complaining bitterly of unseen nettles and brambles.

'I'm all stung. And scratched.'

'Well, I can't help it, can I?' said Paul irritably. 'You don't make such a fuss when it's a picnic or something, do you? There's bound to be nettles in the country.'

'It's not dark on picnics. And it's grass on picnics, not prickles. Anyway, it was last time we went. That one where you got in a bad mood and wouldn't talk to anyone all day and Dad told you off and said you'd spoilt everyone's day and Christine said don't go on at him maybe he's not feeling all that well and . . .'

'Shut up,' said Paul. 'It wasn't like that, anyway.'

'Well, I thought it was. Ouch! It's all muddy in this field, I don't like it.'

Paul shone the torch ahead: there were ridges of sticky plough, breathing out white mist.

'There's a stile over there into another field, and it looks like grass the other side. Come on.'

They followed the hedge for another few yards and climbed the stile.

'Go on,' said Paul. 'Hurry up.'

'What's that little house?'

'It's just a cattleshed.'

'I can hear something inside.'

'Cows.'

'It's a little noise. Cows make big heavy noises.'

'Well, they're little cows, then. Are you ready? I'm going back.'

131

'Coming in a minute. Do you think they're calves?'

'I dunno. Probably. If you want me to help you over the stile you'll have to hurry. I'm off.'

'I like calves. I want to see them.'

'No. Not now.'

'Yes.'

'*No*. Sandra! Come on, can't you? Where are you going? Come back, will you!'

He followed her over black grass, grumbling. The cow-shed was just a shelter, open at one side.

'I can't see in. There is something. Shine the torch, Paul.'

He shone it, and at the same moment a voice said, 'Clear out, you! Put that thing away and beat it, see?'

Sandra retreated behind him and he lowered the torch, but not before it had shown for an instant the two boys crouched together in a corner. Boys older than him, in jeans and black jackets, with licked-back hair and sharp, watching faces. One of them had been holding something he didn't like the look of: a knife, he thought.

'Beat it! And you haven't seen us, see? It's O.K., Mike, they're only kids.'

Paul began to retreat, pulling Sandra with him.

'Here, hang on a minute,' said a different voice. The boy got up and stepped forward, looming in the darkness of the shed. Paul took another step backwards. There were boys like that at school: you kept out of their way. 'You got any money?'

He mumbled: Sandra was tugging at his hand.

'Come on. We won't hurt you. But we're skint, see. And we ain't had nothing to eat all day.'

There was something lodged uncomfortably in the back of Paul's mind: a memory, something he'd heard, something that had to do with this. He said, 'I've got a bit.'

'Come on, then, give us. We wasn't going to hurt you, honest. We thought you was the law, that's all.'

The memory bobbed to the surface. 'The police set up road-blocks today in their search for two ...' 'Couple of blokes in that Mini ... stolen car ...' He dug in his pocket. 'I've got about twenty-five pence. You can have it. I don't need it any more, really, I don't s'pose.'

'Ta. You're a pal. And don't let on you seen us, eh?' The boy had eyes that didn't match the rest of him: they made him look old, but he wasn't.

'No. Did you steal a car?'

'None of your business, is it? Clear off now,' said the other boy.

'Yeah, we did. More'n one. Aw, Ray, they're going to pick us up anyway, aren't they? We'll be back there tomorrow, you can bet your life.'

Paul said, 'Back where?' because he thought he knew already, and had to be sure.

'Back in the nick, mate, that's where.'

He didn't know what to say. How much could he ask, without making them angry? Looking at them, he saw now they were really only two or three years older than he was.

He said, 'Is it a proper one, for men too?'

'Nah. Not when you're under age. They start you off soft, like. Approved School. But we don't approve of it, eh?' He grinned at his companion.

'What do you have to do to get sent there?'

'He done five jobs and I done six. We done probation before, too.'

Probation? 'What sort of jobs?'

'Here,' said the boy roughly. 'What's all this about? I don't like people asking me questions, see? What's it got to do with you?'

Paul said, 'I'm sorry. We'll go now.'

'Yeah. You beat it.'

The other boy said, 'Ta, anyway.'

'It's all right.' Paul hesitated for a moment. 'Best of luck,' he said jerkily. It didn't seem quite right, but he couldn't think of anything else. The boys said nothing, and he backed away from the shed, with Sandra digging her fingers into his arm.

They climbed the stile in silence, the torch cutting a long triangle of light in the darkness. From the other side of the hedge a car's headlights wavered past, and they could hear Bessie cropping the grass.

Sandra said piously, 'Were they naughty boys?'

'Yes. No. I dunno really. I don't know about them.' They'd had funny accents, not from round here. Birmingham, was it? Somewhere like that. And one of them had had eyes that looked as though they knew all about everything, and always had, and didn't think much of it. They'd given him an odd feeling, those eyes: made him want to do something for the boy, help in some way. But you didn't go round offering to help blokes in leather jackets, with knives, did you? You'd soon get told what you could do.

And all the time there was this wonderful feeling of relief flooding over him. The police hadn't been looking for him and Sandra at all: never had been.

'Why did you give them our jug money?' said Sandra.

'I didn't want it any more.' And that was the honest truth. He hadn't wanted it for some time now.

'Oh. Aren't we going to get the padlock either?'

'No. That was a daft idea anyway. Stupid.'

'And not have tea in our room?'

'No,' he said violently. 'No.'

What would happen to those boys? How long would they have to stay in this approved place, if they got taken back there? He was glad he'd given them the money, not that he'd had much choice. He felt guilty at being so happy himself: because that was what he was, at that precise moment, happy.

'Don't say anything to Bill about those boys, Sandra, see?'

'Why not?'

'Just don't, that's all.'

'All right, I won't. Paul?'

'Mmn?'

'*Are* we going to stay at Gran's for always?'

'I dunno really. Why? Do you want to?' What was that funny smell?

'It's just I didn't bring my shell collection. Or my pink hairbrush.'

'They're just things. They don't matter.' It was flowers, that smell. Spring flowers. But it's not spring.

Sandra said nothing, and took her fingers off his arm. He could feel injured dignity burning through the darkness.

'All right. I'm sorry.' You couldn't expect her to understand, not a kid that age. Anyway, maybe she really did have to have them, like, once, a million years ago, he'd had a kind of revolting old rag-thing he'd always taken to bed with him.

He said, 'We can always get them. Anyway, maybe we won't be staying.' It was really most peculiar, but there was a bird singing now. A warbler, pouring out a long, repetitive, exultant song of challenge and invitation.

Birds don't sing in the fog, or at night.

'My shoes are ever so dirty,' said Sandra.

'Never mind. I'll clean them when we get there. Ssh.' It was getting louder and louder, this bird, and the blossom smell, which had begun as an elusive whiff, was quite strong now, and all round. He stared into the white walls of fog until his eyes hurt, and now he could feel warmth on his back as though somewhere there was sunshine, and then suddenly there was someone walking by the hedge, somehow behind the fog: a young woman wearing a blue dress.

It was frustrating, exasperating: she was there, but he could hardly see her. It was like looking into a mirror dimmed by age, or searching for a reflection in a surface of quivering water. He screwed himself into a passion of concentration, fists clenched, shoulders hunched, peering at the elusive figure, and then the fog began to thin, so that she grew clearer and clearer, and quite near, and she was walking in sunshine, on green, thick grass, and there were flowers in the hedges, pink dog-roses and cow-parsley and stitchwort and agrimony and yellow archangel, and the girl was singing.

It was a white dress, he saw now, but so closely patterned with tiny sprigs of blue that it appeared to be blue all over, like a pale summer sky. It was long, down to her ankles, and her brown hair was all coiled and bunched on top of her head. As he watched her she stopped suddenly, sat down on the grass, took off the heavy black boots she wore and walked on in stockinged feet, the boots in one hand. And all the time she was singing away to herself, a song that sometimes had words and sometimes was just a hum: Paul had never seen anyone who so strongly radiated happiness. He was filled with an almost unbearable need to speak to her: to watch was not enough. There was something about her so compelling, something that seemed to have a message for him personally, that he felt tears of anger prick his eyes as he struggled to penetrate the wall between them, the wall that was no wall and yet separated them more surely than a thousand miles. And as he blinked and stared, she turned her head and looked straight at him, and although her face was that of a stranger, there was something in it that he knew, something that again seemed intended just for him, and she looked at him unseeing, but with a bewilderment in her expression, as though there was something she did not understand, as though she, too, struggled to penetrate mystery. And then she shook her head, turned away, and walked on, out of Paul's sight and into the fog which came rolling back into the place where there had been sunshine, flowers, and a young woman walking.

'They're wet, too,' said Sandra. She was still talking about the shoes, he realized.

'We can dry them.' Who was she, that girl? It had been different from the other – messages, or whatever they were – that one.

'I've torn my skirt a bit.'

He looked down. It was the same blue, almost, as the dress the girl had worn. A nice colour. He'd not thought that before.

'It's the one Christine made.'

'I know. I expect Gran can mend it so she won't know.'

Sandra was burrowing at the hedge. 'I can't get through. Please help me. What are you waiting for?'

'Sorry. Coming.' No good hanging about: it had gone now, whatever it had been.

Bill heard them coming and called out, 'You've taken your time, haven't you? I thought you'd taken off for keeps.'

'Sorry. It was muddy and we had to go into the next field.'

'Bessie thought we'd shacked up for the night. Come on then, old girl.'

The cart lurched forward again. The motionless hulks that were the donkeys came to reluctant and protesting life, tripping at the end of their ropes.

Paul said suddenly, 'Are you going on just because of us? Would you have stopped for the night by now otherwise?'

'Maybe. Maybe not. I can pick and choose, eh? Besides, I said I'd see you there safe. We didn't reckon with so many hold-ups.'

'Why's today been longer than most days are?' said Sandra.

Paul said, 'It hasn't. It's just seemed longer. They're all the same really.'

'Maybe she don't mean longer in time,' said Bill. 'Longer in what's happened. Eh? Some days more can happen to you than in the rest of your life put together, can't it?'

'You mean if you're mixed up in a battle or something?'

'It don't have to be anything as big as a battle. It can be something you read in a book, or a conversation you had with someone, or a place you've been to – something like that, not important in itself, but it can hit you smack between the eyes and make you see things quite different all of a sudden. I've known that happen, years ago, and it's stayed with me ever since, so that day seems a week long when I think back on it.'

'What happened?' said Paul.

'It was right back when I was a young man, not long married. It was a bad time, when there wasn't much work to be had, and I was out of a job, and we hadn't much put by, so my wife was worried what would happen, and what with one thing and another we'd had a right good row, to and fro at each other over the kitchen table, and I'd picked up my cap and walked out that morning in as nasty a mood as I've ever been in. I was going after a job I'd heard about at a big house near where we were living then, Something-or-other Hall it was called, and there was some bloke had bought it as people said had just made himself a lot of money in business. And there was this job advertised as a gardener, and being as how I always liked an open-air job I thought it would suit me nicely if I could get it. It wasn't much money, but you couldn't be choosy in those days.

'Anyway, I went up to this place, and a fellow came to the door in a uniform all done up with braid and buttons like he was some kind of soldier, and told me to wait. And then after a while he came back and said the master would see me in the library, and looked at me as though for two pins he'd tell me to take my boots off before I came in, and off we went through this house all tricked out like a museum with statues and pictures, and he pushed me through a door and there I was in this room with the walls all covered with bookshelves, and carpets so deep you felt you were wading through a ploughed field. And at the far end of it there were these two people sitting each side of a table, a man and a woman, having their breakfast, all very grand with silver dishes and that. The man looked up when I came in – a little round chap he was – and waved his hand at me as though to say "Wait", so I stood there by the door and waited, and they went on talking to each other, and I couldn't help hearing, because there was I in the same room.

'And what it was, they were saying one thing to each other, and meaning something else. They were talking all very nice and polite, but underneath it you could hear them hating each other: they were going on and on about some do they'd been to, and the husband was telling his wife she'd let him down, only he didn't say it straight, he wrapped it up in different words, only she understood all right and she was letting him have it right back, with little things she said that sounded fine on top but when you thought about it they were like little sharp arrows. I thought it was funny them letting me hear all this, and then I realized they weren't thinking of me as a person, I mean, not a person like they were, so it was like talking in front of the dog for them. I didn't fancy that: so I tried not to listen, and looked round the room instead. And I got to noticing all the books. Hundreds and hundreds of them there were, great thick leather ones with gold lettering, and I was really envious, I don't mind telling you. I've always been a reading man, and even back then I was always after books, from the penny library, and from second-hand shops, and that. Anyway, I looked at all these books, and I thought: you can keep your house and your big garden and your silver pots and your thick carpets, but those books I'd dearly like to have. And I thought he must be an educated man, to have all those books, and I was envious of that too because I'd not had much education, and that's something else I'd have dearly liked.

'Well, after a bit they stopped talking, and the wife went out of the room. And the man got up and lit himself a cigarette and came towards me. He asked me one or two things to see if I was qualified for the job, like, and I answered him straight, and then he started on about these gardens he had, only he called them grounds, and how he was going to spend hundreds of pounds on them to make them what he called "the finest in the country", and I remember thinking it was odd to talk about money like that to someone like me, and I realized he wouldn't think of that because he couldn't put himself in someone else's place, so to speak, so he couldn't know how I'd feel. And it seemed he had to impress me, make sure I realized he was better than me, and that seemed funny too. I wasn't listening all that carefully, and I couldn't keep my eyes off those books. He must have noticed, because all of a sudden he said, "I see you're looking at my books."

'"You've got some fine books there," I said.

'And he laughed, this little fellow, and he said, "Ah. You

140

have a look at this," and he went over to this great bookcase, and he pressed some kind of button-thing at the side, and the whole of the front swung open, and behind there was just shelves with bottles of drink and glasses, and a gramophone and a lot of records. They weren't books at all, you see, just a fake.

'I s'pose my mouth must have dropped open in astonishment, because he roared with laughter. "Nice little gadget, isn't it?" he said. "Clever."

'I didn't say anything at all. I was shocked, really shocked. It was like putting an axe to a tree and finding it hollow inside – the same kind of let-down feeling. And there was he, pleased as punch with himself. And do you know, I felt sorry for him. Really sorry. Because it came to me all of a sudden that there was he trying so hard to make sure I knew what a lot he'd got, one way and another, and all of a sudden I knew he hadn't got anything, at least not to my way of thinking.

'"Right you are," he said, "I'll take you on. You can start Monday. See the head gardener on your way out."

'And I said, "I'm sorry I've wasted your time, but I don't want the job after all", because you see I knew I couldn't work for a bloke I didn't have any respect for. I couldn't bring myself to say "Sir", either, like you were supposed to in those days.

'And, do you know, it was a queer thing but I went home as happy as a sandboy, even though I'd not got myself a job and things were just back where they'd been before. And I went straight into the house and picked my wife up and I gave her a great hug. "You'll do," I said. "You'll do." She didn't know what I was on about, poor soul, she thought I'd gone off my rocker. I never did tell her what happened: I couldn't have explained it, not put it into words. At least not then.'

'Did you get a job?' said Paul

'Eh? Oh yes, in the end. Not right away, though, we had some hard times. But I got a job as a postman. I was lucky, that was thought a good job then. Secure. And I liked it a lot. It's an independent kind of a job, postman, and it suited me.'

The fog was thicker than ever, rolling back only yards in front of them, so that you felt if you moved any faster you would break into the mass of it and vanish. Paul looked at Sandra and saw she was asleep again. His own eyes burned with tiredness, and his arms and limbs ached with the unaccustomed jolting of the cart, but, for the first time, he felt a curious peace.

He said, 'Are we nearly there?'

'I reckon we can't be far off. Tell you the truth, I've lost my bearings a bit, with this mist. But we can't go wrong if we just keep on, eh?'

'No.'

He closed his eyes. Bessie's hooves hit the tarmac with a solid beat: keep on, keep on, keep on.

They were going through a small village: houses, cottages, a shop, cars huddled on to a grass verge.

'Ah,' said Bill. 'Now I know where we are. There's the police house.'

Police? A small signal of alarm flickered in Paul's mind, and immediately died. He wasn't even worried about them any more: he'd been wrong about all that, quite, quite wrong. It had been one of those times when he'd got himself believing that one thing was happening when really it wasn't at all: he knew now. He'd got that sorted out now.

'It doesn't look like a police station,' he said.

'It isn't. It's just where the local bloke lives. I'll tell you what it used to be, though, that house. It's the old poor-house, I've heard, from way back. That's where all them as were no use had to live, them as couldn't work and had nowhere else to go. Back when every parish had to care for its own poor, you see, and made a right sour job of it as often as not.'

They passed the small, square building and clattered on past silent, curtained houses. The hoofbeats rang in Paul's ears: keep on, keep on, keep on, listen, listen, listen . . .

Listen, master, listen to poor Jennet. Pity poor Jennet, master, pity me, pity, pity, pity . . .

I can hear you, whoever you are – I'm listening – I'll listen. Keep on, keep on, tell me, tell me, I'll listen, listen . . .

She was as thin as a winter tree, with matted hair trailing back from a small face that had perhaps never been quite clean: thin, wasted even, but nonetheless expecting a child because her belly jutted out under her ragged dress, making her sit awkwardly on the horse, leaning a little backwards. And there was another child, small, of indeterminate sex, perched up behind her, clutching on with stick-like arms. They were as clear as daylight to Paul, they, and the horse they rode, and the man with them on the other horse, the grey, and the house they stood before, and the dirty children staring from a gutter. But all the time he could hear the regular beat of Bessie's hooves on the tarmac, and feel, but no longer see, Sandra beside him, and smell the sulphur smell of the fog.

He thought: I am two people, I am now, but I am also, somehow, then.

And the girl who was not now but only then, shifted and put her hand to her back as though something hurt her, and followed with her eyes the man on the grey horse, who was rapping with his stick on the door of the house, scattering the children like chickens.

That is John Harris, Constable, of the Parish of Bletch-ley, who wishes to speak to Thomas Mason, Overseer, of the Parish of Cold Higham, concerning I, Jennet Haynes, Widow, of Nowhere. For it is not allowed that I, and my children, being of Nowhere, stay in the Parish of Bletch-ley, or we shall become chargeable as paupers to the good people of Bletchley, so he returns me to this Parish, which I have told them was the place of settlement of my husband, who is dead. But I, and my child, being of Nowhere, have already been sent out from this Parish last month, and with great haste, lest my new child should be born and there be three of us chargeable upon the Parish, for the Justices have said that my husband's settlement was not a legal settle-ment, and he, too, was of Nowhere.

I must, they say, go to the place of settlement of my father.

I do not know my father's name.

Thomas Mason, Overseer, is saying that he will not take me in, and that if I stay in this Parish I must be whipped as a Vagrant.

It is not permitted to be a Vagrant.

I am a Vagrant, for I am of Nowhere.

John Harris, Constable, is saying that the Parish of Bletchley has already incurred expenses to the total of three pounds two shillings and sixpence for the removal of Jennet Haynes, Widow, of Nowhere.

Thomas Mason, Overseer, replies that this Parish also has paid for the removal of Jennet Haynes, and will pay no more.

A Parish is liable only to feed its own Poor: the Poor who are of Nowhere must go there for their support.

They stood, frozen in the sunlight of another time, the two men looking at the girl with eyes that were not cruel but indifferent: the girl, and the child with eyes like a little

animal and sores on its arms, looking back not with resent-
ment but with numb acceptance of an implacable world.

And then they faded, and there was just the road, and the
fog, and the smack of the hoofbeats: keep on, keep on,
nowhere, nowhere, nowhere . . .

And Sandra's voice saying, 'Why are you crying, Paul?'

IO

'I'm not.' He dragged the sleeve of his anorak across his face, and blinked.

'You were. I could see. You don't ever cry. Dad says that's one of the funny things about you. You didn't cry even when those boys at school took your satchel and mucked all your things about.'

'That just made me angry, didn't it? Not sad.'

'Why are you sad now, then?'

'I didn't say I was.'

She peered closely at him. 'There's still wetness on your face.'

He scowled, and glanced at Bill. The old man was not listening, sitting with his head tucked down into his chest.

'Oh, shut up, Sandra. Anyway, it's not so awful. Even grown-ups cry sometimes.'

'Do they? When?'

'When they're sad, I s'pose.'

'Then you're sad?'

He didn't answer. That was the best way when she started going on like that, otherwise you got all agitated and ended up shouting at her. She couldn't help it really, all little kids do it, don't they?

'Are you sad because Dad might tell you off?'

'What? No.'

'Will he?'

'Will he what?'

'You're not listening to me. Will Dad tell you off?'

146

'I don't know. Probably. Anyway it isn't anything to do with that.'

Nothing to do with me at all really. But it was. Because things are if you can feel them, aren't they?

He pointed at the ditch beside the road, to distract her. 'Look!' There was a hedgehog, caught for a moment in the light of the lantern, trundling like a little tank among the dead leaves.

Will he tell me off? Yes. Stands to reason, doesn't it? They must've been worried sick, he and Christine. And when you've been worried you get angry: it's only natural. But the funny thing is I don't think I'll mind. It'll be a kind of relief, somehow.

I'm so tired, he thought, I feel as though we'd been about a hundred miles. This morning feels a million years ago, come to that.

He closed his eyes and leaned back against the sacks. He let pieces of the day come floating into his mind, as snatches of sound, pictures, feelings: the manager in the shop saying, 'Let's see what you've got in your pocket' to a boy who seemed, now, almost like someone else; rooks croaking above the valley where those people had fought the Danes, and died; Bessie's hooves smacking down on the road; hedges burning with colour against the fog; a woman in a cottage, holding a dead hare in her hand; Matthew Cobham, a plain and private man; a shadow on a wall, the chink of a stirrup, a hoarse voice talking in the darkness; boys in a shed, with hard eyes.

Other people.

Listening to other people.

You think everything's happening just to you, he thought, but it isn't. It's happening to other people too. It sounds obvious when you say it, but it isn't till you think

147

about it. Me and Christine: it's been happening to her too. Only I haven't ever listened to her.

I've been like someone with a bad cold, all kind of shut up inside myself, not being able to hear other people. Just shouting out at them sometimes.

The cart jolted over a stone and he sat up with a jerk, opening his eyes. There were lights ahead, glittering through the dark. Something felt different, too.

'Hey! The fog's gone.'

'Yes,' said Bill. 'Funny stuff, fog. You can run slap into a bank of it and then right out again a few miles farther on, like it had never been there.'

'Where are we?'

'Don't you know?'

'No.'

'This is Cold Higham, son. End of the trip, far as you're concerned.'

He could see the outlines of houses now, hard and substantial. They looked real, without the floating quality bestowed on everything by the mist. The feeling of unreality he'd had himself all day seemed to have gone too. For the first time since he'd stood in the shop, that morning, holding that padlock and chain, he felt quite ordinary. Tired, but ordinary.

'You'll be glad to get to your Gran's, I daresay, and off the road.'

'What did you say it was called, this road? The what?'

'The Driftway.'

'It was what you said. A place that's got messages. I know now.'

'I told you, didn't I? Think yourself lucky. They're not there for everyone.'

'What are you talking about?' said Sandra. 'Are we there yet?'

'Almost. It makes you feel as though you'd been much farther than you have really. I mean, as though you'd not gone just so many miles along a road, but moved around in all sorts of other ways as well. Weird, really.'

'Oh, aye.'

'It's not something you could tell people about.'

'I daresay not,' said Bill. 'Where does your Gran live, then?'

'Oh, yes. It's the last one of that row of cottages past the church.'

It was raining. The road shone, patterned with rings of yellow light reflected in puddles.

'What'll you do?' said Paul. 'I mean, when you've dropped us off?'

'We'll shack up for the night. There's a field farther on where the farmer's not one of those choosy fellows as'll turn me off after half an hour.'

'It's such a beastly night. I'm sure my Gran . . .'

'Look, son,' said Bill. 'I chose how I live, didn't I? But thanks all the same.'

He could see the light in her window now: blue, because the curtains were blue. They had lighter blue flowers on them and she'd had them ever since he could remember. He said, 'Could you drop us off just before, please? I want to ask the lady next door to tell her we're here, so she doesn't get a fright.'

'Whoa there, Bessie! Hold up, then. This do?'

'Yes, thank you.'

He slid down from the cart: lifted Sandra off.

'You'd best get in out of the wet, son. Not just stand there.'

'Yes.' Bessie twitched an ear, and silver drops sprayed into the night. Bill was filling his pipe with that reeking tobacco, the reins slung over his arm.

'Something wrong?'

'No. Nothing. Just . . . Well, thank you very much for the lift.'

'Don't mention it. I told you I don't mind a bit of company from time to time. We had a good chat, eh?'

'I'll say.'

'Well, I'll be on my way, then.' He picked up the reins. The donkeys jerked their heads and laid their ears back. 'Get up, there!'

'If you're ever in Banbury,' said Paul, 'it's 14 Ladymead Crescent.'

'Ah. Drop in for a cup of tea, is that it?'

'Yes. If you'd like to.'

'What about that Christine of yours?'

'It'll be all right,' said Paul. 'I'll have told them about you. Her, too.'

'Maybe I will, then.'

'Well, good-bye. Thanks very much.'

'Cheero, son.'

The cart moved away. For a while Paul could still see the old man's hunched shoulders and the red gleam of the lantern: then they vanished into the darkness and he could only hear the noise of Bessie's hooves on the road: then that, too, was gone.

Sandra said resignedly, 'I'm just getting wetter and wetter. Why are we staying out here?'

'Sorry.' He took his eyes away from the road. There were other things to be thought about now. First of all, whatever anybody said to him there wasn't to be any getting into a temper and going off in a sulk: because he'd been a right dope from the beginning, and that was a fact. And he'd have to remember that, through all the things that were going to be said, and keep a hold of himself. That manager in the shop had been wrong to jump on them like that, but if he'd been sensible with the woman policeman, every-thing would have been all right. There hadn't been any need to go rushing off: it was as though he'd grabbed hold of what had happened as some kind of excuse . . .

He decided not to go on thinking about that: there wasn't any point, was there? 'Come on. Let's see if Mrs Lang is in.'

She opened the door at once in answer to his knock. 'Ah, Paul. Your Gran'll be glad to see you. She's not gone out, you know.'

It wasn't the reaction he'd expected: she hadn't been surprised to see them. But it would be best to get straight on in to Gran's, not stop to ask questions. He thanked her, and they went up the brick path to Gran's house.

He let Sandra run in first, and followed more slowly. He could hear her chattering, and Gran saying things in her deeper voice, before he opened the kitchen door. He stood there, waiting for her to be astonished, angry, questioning: she only said, 'You look wet through. Shall I do you some soup or would you rather have a cup of tea?'

He said, 'Soup, please,' and sat at the table while she moved about the room. She didn't say much: just a few things about Sandra having lost her hair-ribbons, and her shoes being in a shocking mess.

'We went in a field. There were some boys . . .'

Paul said, 'Oughtn't we to let Dad and Christine know we're here?' He had to look away while he was saying it: keep his eyes on that old photo on the dresser of Grandad in his army uniform, and Gran when she was young.

'That's been seen to.'

He turned round, amazed. 'They know? You knew we were coming here then?'

'Well, it was obvious, wasn't it, dear? Your Dad went to

see the police when you didn't get home, and they said there were these two children had run off from Hatterson's shop, they put two and two together, and then not long after that I had a message from the police here that he'd heard you were coming along with someone he knew and you were in good hands, and he got a message back to your Dad. You'll be stopping here the night now, and go back on the bus tomorrow.'

There was a silence: the clock ticked: Sandra was hunting in the dresser cupboard for the biscuit tin. 'Is Dad cross?'

'He won't be best pleased, I daresay. You'll have to say you're sorry.'

'Yes, I know. We didn't take those things in the shop, Gran.'

'No. We never thought that.'

'How did the police know who we were with, though?'

'Well, the person had a word with a policeman at some point, I think. He thought we'd be worried, see. It was thoughtful of him.'

It would have been back where that accident was. And he never said a word. Crafty. It could have felt like a betrayal, but didn't.

'You were a long time coming, though,' said Gran. 'It's not so far, after all.'

'Yes. It was a cart, you see, not a car. And we went off the main road for one bit, along the old road. It's called the Driftway.'

'I know the Driftway,' said Gran. 'I've been along there myself, way back, oh, a long time ago. Here's your soup, then.'

'Thank you.' He'd been looking at that old picture of her again, because there was something about it that nagged him. She'd had long hair then, and he'd never noticed that

152

before, but it wasn't that. He got up and went over to the dresser, picked it up, and stared.

'Was this dress white, Gran? With little blue bits on it?'

'That's right. How did you know that, for goodness sake! It was my best: I was so proud of it.'

The dress: but even more than that, the face. Happy, looking straight at him on a sunny, summer day. He said, 'Did you wear it once walking along that road?'

'So I did! It was when I got the news your Grandad was back from the war, in nineteen seventeen. He'd been wounded, you see, and they sent him home for good: it was when we were engaged. When I got the news I was so happy I couldn't wait to see him and I put on my best dress and I walked all the way to where he lived then: nearly seven miles. I can remember it so well: it was a beautiful day with all the summer flowers out, and I remember I thought it was the best day of my life, and I sang to myself, and took my boots off and walked barefoot in the grass.'

He said, 'I know,' but she didn't hear, busy hustling Sandra to the sink, to wash her face and hands.

'What we all wondered, Paul, was what you were doing going down to that shop in the first place? What was it you wanted there?'

'Just some things. At least I thought I did. I don't any more now. We won't be going there any more.'

Sandra twisted her face round under Gran's arm. 'Not the jug, Paul? Aren't we getting the jug any more? And the brush and that?'

He said, 'No. We don't want them any more.'

'Oh, I see.' She bent over the sink again, docile.

'Well, you know best,' said Gran. She was unbuttoning Sandra's dress.

'You'd better be getting up to bed. It's late. I've put the folding bed up for you.'

'Yes. When's the bus tomorrow?'

'They'll be expecting you on the half past ten. Only your Dad won't be in when you get back: he's got to work tomorrow. But Christine'll be waiting in for you.'

'Oh, I see.'

He knew what he was going to do. He'd go straight into the kitchen, and he'd get his coat hung up, and then, however difficult it was and even if he didn't want to by then, he'd say, 'Hello, Christine.'

He thought he would want to, probably.

FANNY AND THE MONSTERS

Three delightful stories about the irrepressible Fanny, who is expected to lead the life of a demure Victorian girl but whose spirit and sense of adventure constantly lead her into trouble of one sort or another!

THE REVENGE OF SAMUEL STOKES

What on earth was happening on the new housing estate? Washing machines smelling of roast venison, tobacco smoke coming out of television sets, greenhouses turning into Greek temples – it was enough to make Tim and Jane think that a malign spirit was at work!

THE GHOST OF THOMAS KEMPE

Strange messages, fearful noises and all kinds of jiggery-pokery . . . It began to dawn on James that there was probably a ghost in the house. But what kind of ghost was it that had come to plague the Harrison family in their lovely old cottage? (Winner of the Carnegie Medal)

THE WILD HUNT OF HAGWORTHY

The ancient Horn Dance was a tradition which had been left buried for hundreds of years, and best left buried, muttered some of the older villagers. Lucy, visiting her aunt for the first time in five years, was to discover the dark secret of the Horn Dance, the ghostly Wild Hunt which lay behind it – and the terrible danger which came with it . . .

ASTERCOTE

The village of Astercote has been overgrown by forest but its past still haunts the local Cotswold folk, as Peter and Mair discover. A tense and eerie story.

THE HOUSE IN NORHAM GARDENS

'Step back into the past,' said Clare. 'In this house we preserve an older, finer way of life. Welcome to nineteen thirty-six.' And in the huge Victorian house she discovers a vividly painted shield from New Guinea and becomes obsessed with its past . . .

A STITCH IN TIME

This seaside holiday is a time of finding things for Maria: names for birds and wild flowers, fossils in the Dorset rocks, a new friend, Martin, a different Maria who likes noisy games and a little girl called Harriet who lived in this holiday house a hundred years ago, and sewed an elaborate sampler – but why didn't she finish it?

THE WHISPERING KNIGHTS

William and Susie thought they were just playing when they cooked up a witches' brew in the old barn and chanted a spell over it, but they found they'd raised a dark and hostile force from a time far older than their own . . .

UNINVITED GHOSTS

Try telling your mother that you can't sleep because there's a ghost in the room clacking its needles and humming. Or that there's a Martian at the front door. Or that there's a dragon living underneath the house. She'll never believe you. But strange things do happen and these ingenious tales show just how extraordinary life can be.

GOING BACK

This is a book about remembering. On going back to Medleycott, the adored home of her childhood, Jane is flooded with memories of those happy and idyllic times. So what was it that induced Jane and her brother Edward to run away from the place they both loved so intensely?

A HOUSE INSIDE OUT

Next time you find a wood-louse in the bath, think twice before you wash it down the waste-pipe – it may be on a dangerous and thrilling mission!

More books from Puffin

WOOF!
Allan Ahlberg

Eric is a perfectly ordinary boy. Perfectly ordinary, that is, until the night when, safely tucked up in bed, he slowly turns into a dog! Fritz Wegner's drawings illustrate this funny and exciting story superbly.

VERA PRATT AND THE FALSE MOUSTACHES
Brough Girling

There were times when Wally Pratt wished his mum was more ordinary and not the fanatic mechanic she was, but when he and his friends find themselves caught up in a real 'cops and robbers' affair, he is more than glad to have his mum, Vera, to help them.

SADDLEBOTTOM
Dick King-Smith

Hilarious adventures of a Wessex Saddleback pig whose white saddle is in the wrong place, to the chagrin of his mother.

SLADE
John Tully

Slade has a mission – to investigate life on Earth. When Eddie discovers the truth about Slade he gets a whole lot more adventure than he bargained for.

A TASTE OF BLACKBERRIES
Doris Buchanan Smith

The moving story about a young boy who has to come to terms with the tragic death of his best friend and the guilty feeling that he could somehow have saved him.

THE PRIME MINISTER'S BRAIN
Gillian Cross

The fiendish DEMON HEADMASTER plans to gain control of No. 10 Downing Street and lure the Prime Minister into his evil clutches.

JASON BODGER AND THE PRIORY GHOST
Gene Kemp

A ghost story, both funny and exciting, about Jason, the bane of every teacher's life, who is pursued by the ghost of a little nun from the twelfth century!

HALFWAY ACROSS THE GALAXY AND TURN LEFT
Robin Klein

A humorous account of what happens to a family banished from their planet Zygron, when they have to spend a period of exile on Earth.

SUPERGRAN TO THE RESCUE
Forrest Wilson

The punchpacking, baddiebiffing escapades of the world's No. 1 senior citizen superhero – Super Gran! Now a devastating series on ITV!

TOM TIDDLER'S GROUND
John Rowe Townsend

Vic and Brain are given an old rowing boat which leads to the unravelling of a mystery and a happy reunion of two friends. An exciting adventure story.

JELLYBEAN
Tessa Duder

A sensitive modern novel about Geraldine, alias 'Jellybean', who leads a rather solitary life as the only child of a single parent. She's tired of having to fit in with her mother's busy schedule, but a new friend and a performance of 'The Nutcracker Suite' change everything.

THE PRIESTS OF FERRIS
Maurice Gee

Susan Ferris and her cousin Nick return to the world of O which they had saved from the evil Halfmen, only to find that O is now ruled by cruel and ruthless priests. Can they save the inhabitants of O from tyranny? An action-packed and gripping story by the author of prize-winning *The Halfmen of O*.

THE SEA IS SINGING
Rosalind Kerven

In her seaside Shetland home, Tess is torn between the plight of the whales and loyalty to her father and his job on the oil rig. A haunting and thought-provoking novel.

BACK HOME
Michelle Magorian

A marvellously gripping story of an irrepressible girl's struggle to adjust to a new life. Twelve-year-old Rusty, who had been evacuated to the United States when she was seven, returns to the grey austerity of post-way Britain.

THE BEAST MASTER
Andre Norton

Spine-chilling science fiction – treachery and revenge! Hosteen Storm is a man with a mission to find and punish Brad Quade, the man who killed his father long ago on Terra, the planet where life no longer exists.